Advance Praise for *Eat, Sleep, Love*

"With keen attention and urgent affection, Chuck Forester brings to life the San Francisco of the 1970s and early 1980s, and the band of gay brothers who came together with 'thundering exhilarations, billows of joy,' and 'consuming lust.' 'Great sex flows like a mighty river,' declares this novel's hero Charlie. As Forester goes on to evoke the impossible pain those brothers suffered in the age of AIDS, he deepens his gratitude for a lifetime of man-to-man pleasures, and ultimately, he champions the power and profound possibilities of gay desire. *Eat, Sleep, Love* vividly celebrates men who commit to living fully in the body."

—David Groff, author of *Clay*

"Much more than a coming out story. Set in the embrace of the groundbreaking and extraordinarily inventive San Francisco gay culture of the 1970s. This is a moving, evocative tale of Charlie's love, loss, sex, and coming into his own. A fascinating book that follows colorful characters and absorbing adventures unique to that time period and beyond what many know today. A particularly engaging chapter is 'The Makings of a Fine Sex Date,' which is great reading, and how-to sex manual for anyone, not just those who hmcave just recently come out. Recommended reading!"

—Michael Samuel, former board member,
Lambda Literary Foundation

"Charlie's youth in Point Reyes, is the best-executed passage. The how-to manual for gay men is much needed. The chapter titled 'Touch Me, Remind Me Who I Am,' contains the insights and wisdom you've accumulated over the decades."

—Edwin Bayrd, author and editor

Praise for *Our Time*

"Forester captures San Francisco in a way few have—he gives us the grit, the excess and the adventure, but also the magic and wonder that made the city a once upon a time. It really is a very inspired piece of writing, so honest, so real."
—Trebor Healey, author of *A Horse Named Sorrow*

"Chuck's romp through his coming out in 1970s San Francisco is more than just a single guy on the loose, it's the narrative of the building of a movement."
—Jewelle Gomez, author of *The Gilda Stories*

"Chuck Forester adroitly captures the sexualized zeitgeist of San Francisco in the early 1970s, as gay men flocked there to find themselves, each other, and created new unabashed futures together."
—John R. Killacky, Executive Director, Flynn Center for the Performing Arts

Eat
Sleep
Love

Also by the author

Do You Live Around Here?

Our Time: San Francisco in the '70s

Eat
Sleep
Love

A novel

Chuck Forester

Querelle Press
New York, NY

Published by Querelle Press LLC
2808 Broadway #4
New York, NY 10025

www.querellepress.com

ISBN 978-1-7335980-0-2 (paper edition)
ISBN 978-1-7335980-1-9 (e-book edition)

Printed in the United States
Cover design by Linda Kosarin/The Art Department
Typeset by Raymond Luczak

This novel is dedicated to the young men who found that sex made them a better person and not to those who didn't.

"I sing the body electric."
—Walt Whitman

Contents

Preface 1

1: Let Your Dreams Outgrow 5

2: First Taste of the City 14

3: Christopher Robin 19

4: Never Stop Believing 23

5: There's No Love Like the First 34

6: Twins 42

7: Company Town 49

8: New Man in Town 55

9: The Makings of a Fine Sex Date 62

10: Awakening 72

11: Only You Can Only Give Me That Feeling 77

12: Love Is Not a Victory March 83

13: Nothing Good Lasts Forever 88

14: We All Make Mistakes 95

15: Enough! 101

16: Remembering the Dead 106

17: Touch Me, Remind Me Who I Am 118

18: A Man and His Dog 123

19: The Past Beats Inside Me 134

Author's Note 136

Acknowledgments 138

About the Author 139

Preface

The protagonist of this story, Charlie McKey, is a sexually active HIV-positive gay man who comes from a small coastal California town. After the AIDS-related death of his partner, he finds a way of loving another man in a way he never imagined. His story includes a fair amount of sex, so if his story isn't your cup of tea, please pass it on to someone else because there aren't many stories like this one floating around the queer cosmos.

In the time before AIDS, gay men thrilled at being able to hold hands in public and there were lovers that tripped on psilocybin mushrooms in a sacred grove of redwoods. The only disease they worried about was VD, and they were healed six days after getting shots at the city's anonymous free clinic.

There is no place like San Francisco, and this story is about San Francisco's attitude-altering era beginning in the early 1970s, when the city, emptied of the middle class, was descended upon by gay men who were going to live any damn way they wanted. It especially attracted sexually active men like Charlie, who had the most to gain because they could have sex without an iota of shame.

South of Market after dark was their playground, with leather bars for the serious as well as for the sisters. The men at the Stud opened their minds with LSD and turned sheds behind Victorians into hobbits' cottages. There was a bathhouse for the suit crowd and another bathhouse for the young and frivolous. There was also a sex club for fist-fuckers and the ultimate pleasure palace, the Hothouse, was designed for serious sex by serious players.

Around Castro Street, gay bars popped up overnight like mushrooms. The bartenders at the Midnight Sun and Moby Dick were like rock stars, and Toad Hall, now Walgreen's, was popular with horny, hoodie-under-denim-jacket men, and it had a line the went around the corner on Sundays. There was a bar for blacks and their friends, and there was another bar for the "nothing specials." There were more than seventy bars in the city and the baths were scattered, so depending on his craving on a given day, Charlie satisfies his on his way home from work. If he doesn't go to the movies, he has sex with a buddy or with someone he hooked up with at a bar.

Men moved around frequently because the real estate market was as loose as a bowl of Jell-O. They changed apartments because a bigger or a better apartment or home became available, and the best ones changed hands by word of mouth, and sometimes by the man you slept with. Even though some gay men couldn't talk about their sexuality at work, they were eternally grateful to live in the only city in America where they could be themselves.

Charlie grows up in Point Reyes Station, where there are limits on what he can do and say, and that attitude permeates everything he does, but when he looks around San Francisco he finds no walls because there aren't any. The shock knocks him backwards because he doesn't think that a city of such out and out freedom could possibly exist. Charlie is eager to sample San Francisco's many troves of pleasures, the dark alleys of passion and the exotic. If that freedom overwhelmed someone, they often turned to drugs—or they went back to where they came from.

Since this is a gay novel, you want to know how much and

what kind of sex is included. San Francisco is Auntie Mame's banquet, and Charlie doesn't starve! He goes for the suckling pig! When he likes a drug, he does it again, and when he has fun with a man in bed, he makes a second date with him. In a warm bath of men finding being themselves is easier than being in the closet, Charlie falls in love with Enos, who shows him the quick rich tech world as the city of the 1970s morphs into the '80s, and San Francisco takes a new and deadly turn.

Chapter One

"Let your dreams outgrow the shoes of your expectations."
—Ryunosuke Satoro, poet

1971

Point Reyes Station kept me apart from Northern California and light years from the action in the rest of America. I was eleven when a semi jackknifed on a rainy night, and the hurling cab crushed Mom and Pops' Buick. The two hours that began when Mom said that she was going to the movies and I could go on my next birthday are etched forever in memory as the worst hours of my life. That night she drove off as casual as Donna Reed and blew me kisses before turning and disappearing. An hour later, Pops said, "I never wanted to ever have to say this, Mom is dead." He broke down with his body shaking. Pops was a local boy. The only time I felt close to him were the times when from his father's faded, leather chair, he regaled me with the sea faring yarns he'd told me since I was learning to read.

Mom was my anchor, starting every day fresh with a smile. That day, I magically thought that if I could stop Pops crying, she would come back from the movies. I put my hand on his arm and said, "Everything's going to be fine." He looked at me like he didn't know me, and I started bawling. Once I got started, get ready for a storm because there would be hours of thunder. The hurt lasted a year and continued to simmer thereafter.

Pops got a degree at a trade school, bragging that his real education was the boats in Tomales Bay. His little office on the dock had tide charts on the wall, and he knew every boat that came within a quarter mile of the bay. During the day, Pops was on his boat and at night, at the bar swapping stories with fishermen. The townsfolk called him the harbormaster; I called him my sad absent father. He was as devastated by Mom's loss as I was, but there was a distance between us.

I never saw relatives, even when most of them lived within twenty minutes of us, because they'd been feuding since Mom and Pops were married. Mom's parents complained that Mom married beneath her. Pops' parents complained that Mom's parents were tight-fisted sonsofbitches that didn't marry her off properly.

I didn't give a shit about religion, and a funeral is the worst of it. The only good thing about Mom's was that it was held in a wood and stucco church across the road from Mom's family ranch outside of Cotati. I spent summers on the ranch as a kid climbing the trees in the orchard and in the fall, stepping carefully among the spawning salmon that turned the stream black with life. I was happy whenever I was on the ranch, and I jacked off for the first time in the barn. The day of the funeral, despite a blazing sun, my relatives were dressed in depressing black, so that I couldn't tell who was from Mom's side and who was Pops' side, not that I cared. All I cared about was them interfering with me, saying goodbye to the mother who hugged me all the time and told me, "You have a spark, Charlie. Cherish it."

The last thing I needed was being surrounded by a gaunt, stained-glass Jesus curing lepers, riding a donkey into Jerusalem, conferring with his disciples, and being baptized by

Paul. In the biggest window, behind a redwood altar, Jesus rose from a rock in what looked like a jock strap with Technicolor spears of light and golden clouds. The service felt like it ran the entire afternoon. I had to pee, and every time I got up, Granny Margaret smacked me smartly with her purse. The pastor's monotone sounded the same to me, and the only time he stopped talking was to catch his breath after saying, "Jesus!" He said "Jesus!" so often, I thought he had a breathing problem. People go to funerals to get closure with the person who died, but this pastor, with slicked back hair and fat hands hunched over the altar, gave the same sermon for everyone who died. He just inserted a new name at the end. What a shitty way to honor my mother!

She was the center of a life that included the cafe and the miles of sand and the acres of pine and scrub growth on Point Reyes. I tried to keep my shit together, but that afternoon after the service ended, the men in the family pretended they were the Kennedys playing touch football in the parking lot. I wanted to knee those SOBs in the groin. I had no patience with the women either. They shoved plates of super rich cakes and plates with fruit-packed pies in my face until I hid in a closet. Did they ever think about why we are there?

The worst of the reception was near the end, when Grandma Godfrey condemned Mom's "special condition." I realized that I'd been witnessing my family's homophobia. Naïve and ignorant, I couldn't understand that Mom could be a lesbian, I thought she was like the other women who had woman friends. My relatives disdain for her tore at my soul, but I kept my peace even though I wanted to scream, "You inconsiderate assholes!" How can people who praise Jesus be so quick to condemn, sweet loving Mom with their indifference?

I learned more hanging around the fishermen living at the mercy of the sea than I did at Pushkin Elementary. In John Muir High School, my English teacher, O. Sloane, was a real oddball, but he was the first man I trusted. He had a ridiculous man-bun piece and his usual outfit was white slacks and blue and white striped Greek sailor shirts to make us think that he hobnobbed with movie stars in Monaco. The day was hot for spring when once I'd broken the rules by wearing shorts to class. When Mr. Sloane said he was taking me out of class, I was sure I was going to the principal's office, a cramped room with a big oak desk where I'd been berated for being a smartass by Mr. Stewart, the principal, more than once. I breathed a sigh of relief when we didn't stop at his door. Instead Mr. Sloane kept walking until he could sneak me into the teacher's lounge. Once he was sure no one could hear him, he confessed that he'd had sex in a stall in a men's room in Grand Central station. When he got home that night, he told his wife that he was going out for a carton of milk, but he never returned. He slipped me his copy of Wilfred Owen's poetry before sneaking unnoticed out of the lounge. Did Mr. Sloane know I wanted to cross the bridge? Was he urging me to do it?

I saved my allowance so I could buy used books about ancient Greek statues and their sculptors because they epitomized male beauty. On the days Pops didn't come home for dinner, I put one of those books on the kitchen table and I imagined talking with the sculptor over dinner about beauty and the male form. Each finely chiseled man was a story of strength and beauty that I memorized so I could recall them when I was down. They became friends that would get me through life.

I felt like a tule elk in Miami the one time in high school I asked a girl, "Would you like to go the movies?" Susie Giamonte was a big girl with strong arms, and I knew she was only being polite when she said yes. But she never shared her giant box of buttered popcorn.

I was never going to be straight, but something deep inside told me the men in nearby San Francisco were going to show me how to live as a gay man. I don't know where it came from, but I knew they would. It still continued to amaze me that a kid from a broken home in Point Reyes Station had that confidence.

San Francisco was my destiny, and I'd put it off too long. If I didn't go now, I never would. I would end up like the boys I went to school with. I'd be a fisherman spending weeks in cramped quarters at sea. When the fish were coming, I'd work to exhaustion hauling one humongous tuna after another into the hold of the boat as fast as I could. The life of a seaman was romantic to a kid, but when I saw the toll that a life at sea had taken on the faces of the men that I saw when I was a teenage waiter at the café, I knew the sea would never be my life. I was made for better things.

I was bundled with questions. I wasn't going to be gay like the actor Charles Nelson Reilly who I'd seen on TV, but who would I be? Would the men in San Francisco like me in jeans? I'd heard gay men raped boys. From the way they said the word rape, it sounded pretty terrible. But if it was what I thought it was and they did it gently, I was all for it when it came to me.

Sex was something people didn't like talking about. At home, it was verboten. The only time sex was mentioned at school was the time coach Bussey told the health class, "Keep it in your knickers." Sex was going to be a magical mystery tour. Every time I jacked off, I imagined living where naked men swam in streams. When they were on dry land, they made the perfect breakfast of sausage links, a rasher of bacon, hash brown potatoes, and sunny side eggs. Call me a carnivore, but if someone made that breakfast for me, I'd love them every day.

Ollie, a year older and the sweeper on the soccer team, gave me gay porno magazines that he was done with. He wrapped them in brown paper from a torn grocery bag and tied them with string so it looked like something bought at Mr. Orson's store. Just to be safe, I kept them inside my jacket when I rode home on my bike. That much free porn and teenage testosterone is volatile. Even before I finished going through the first magazine's soiled pages of naked men in cowboy gear, my imagination careened off every wall in my room. How could there be so much luscious, touchable beauty? Point Reyes Station had none of it. Forget relatives; they were as dull as paste. Point Reyes Station was one of nature's finest works, but for a queer boy, it was a desert.

I spent hours with a magazine open before me on the chenille bedspread. As sun bathed the page with light, I lingered with my favorite model because his face looked honest. As I stared, his eyes seemed to move. He was looking at me, asking me to join him. Even though I knew I could find him there anytime, when I turned the page, the separation punched me in the gut. His faced stayed with me all day. I saw him over my shoulder when I was brushing my teeth. That night I think it was him I saw in my dream, but there was so much haze in the crowded space of my dream that it was hard to see.

My favorite was a blond, who, when seen from the side, looked like a surfer dude. I imagined him chopping down trees and displaying his equipment for me, lying on dock. We did the dishes together after dinners and I wrote him a love letter that I never sent because the magazine didn't identify the address of the company that published it. I kept the letter under my pillow until I decided that was silly.

I opened another magazine the next day, and a dark-haired man with adequate equipment became my new favorite because the warmth of his smile was genuine. We bought a home together and got a dog. I opened the rest of the magazines, but I never looked at my first favorite again because I couldn't bear his look of disappointment.

The hardcore magazine that I saved for last featured men having anal sex. It was the first tune I saw men fucking, with a curled-up man being fucked by a man who curled around him. They intrigued me. I thought about what it would feel like and wondered if I'd scream like a girl it if hurt. I couldn't see their faces but I could tell from the way they were joined that fucking was a wondrous thing. I had to know more about it.

A couple times when I was showering, I stuck my finger in my ass, and that excited me, but I waited a month before I got up the courage to ask Ollie if he had ever been fucked. That was not something you're supposed to ask a friend, but I was obsessed. Ollie said, "Fucking is God's gift to gay men." At first I thought he was joking, but when he described the first time a man fucked him, I knew he wasn't joking. That made for huge expectations.

I knew when I left town that I would miss the summer days on Grandpa's ranch, and that I was never going to be that kid again. Leaving home hurt badly, and I wondered if I had to hurt more before I became a man.

Pops said like a broken record, "You'll never be man until you have your own boat." The priest said, "Sex is a sin." Their words haunted me, but I thought I was ready to cross the bridge to San Francisco. But before I crossed it, I had to get things in order. I wondered if the men in San Francisco would like me, but I was embarrassed to be thinking about that because men weren't supposed to have feelings.

The first hurdle was telling Pops that I was leaving, and then I had to decide what to take with me. I was afraid of what Pops was going to say, so instead of sitting down and talking calmly to him, I began making lists of what I would take. They became an obsession. I made lists of books. I made a list of socks and boots. I ripped that list up and made a list of clothing from the top down, starting with my knit cap, moving down to my blue graduation blazer, the Christmas present cable-stitch sweater, two flannel shirts that I'd had for years and further down six pair of Fruit of the Loom underwear, wool and cotton socks, my brown Oxfords and the work boots that I was going to buy. I woke in the middle of the night and raced to my desk and amended the list to include a pair of chinos and jeans. In the morning when I went over the list, I realized I'd never be able to get all of that into a suitcase and I tore up the list. Was I ever going to have what it took to get me to San Francisco?

I kept coming up with the right words in my head to tell Pops that I was leaving him, but even when they sounded like the words that would let me leave without Pops going ballistic, they didn't sound as good the next day. I had to face it; I couldn't confront him.

By the end of summer I was pissed at myself. But not having the balls to tell Pops I was leaving, I turned it on me. That sent me deep into depression.

Ollie and I stopped on our way back from Duck Beach. I leaned my bike against a tree but when Ollie rested his against brush it couldn't hold it and his bike fell on its side, kicking up dust. "You said you wanted to talk about something," Ollie said, dusting off his hands.

"I'm thinking about crossing the Golden Gate Bridge."

"You mean to San Francisco? It's full of weirdos."

"Yeah but what about the gay men?"

"Are you thinking of moving there?"

"I gotta get away. Pops is driving me crazy."

"What's he up to this time?" Ollie asked as he pulled a long strand of grass and sucked it.

"He's never home."

"Did you see the hippie commune?"

"The what?"

"They have free weed. I mean they welcome everyone. This is their third year, so they grow almost all of their food and they go into town with food stamps for the basics like flower, sugar, and rice. During the day, they play the guitar and sing. You can stay overnight and sit in their healing circle."

"Do you think I'm ready for a big city?"

"How the hell would I know?" he said, spitting out the grass.

"But do you think I'm ready to be gay full-time?"

"I hear you can't even find a place to park there."

"You're the only person who knows I'm gay, so you gotta tell me I'm ready." My anxiety was close to breaking.

"What did you dad say?"

"He'd go ballistic."

"I don't get that old coot.

The wind came up, so Ollie got on his bike. I got my bike

and rode back into town, pissed that Ollie didn't answer my question, because leaving home scared the shit out of me.

The line of ants in glistening black made a perfect crescent around the toe of my shoe. They came from my left, but from where I was sitting outside the café waiting for the bus and looking off in the distance, I couldn't see where they were headed.

"Excuse me, can I sit?" A young mother with her child strapped to her chest towered over me,

"Please. Where are you going?" I asked as she swept grit off the bench and sat, adjusting her child.

"I going back to clean out the house. My dad died."

"I'm so sorry. Was it the house you grew up in?" I asked, hoping she'd say something good about San Francisco.

"The first time I went back I didn't recognize the neighborhood. Redevelopment tore through it like a tornado. You'd think it was one of those cartoons where the house goes poof with one of those white clouds and disappears." She giggled imagining it.

"I am going to San Francisco," I said too forcefully.

"There's a shooting every day. What would you do that?" she asked.

"Is it that dangerous?" My hands were shaking.

"I'm selling the house as fast as I can because I'm not raising my daughter where she can't go out and play with her friends. What's a kid gonna do if they can't get to a park? You know what they're gonna do? They'll end up doing drugs; that's what they'll do. And besides, I saw people of every color you can think of in Safeway the last time I was there. The city ain't the same."

The bus pulled up and stopped. Riders got off and claimed their bags. I started to get up, but I stopped short, saying to myself, "I'm not ready." I crushed the ticket in my hand and walked home, head bowed and pissed that I didn't have the balls to stand up to Pops. I was so caught up in it that I stepped on the ants' mouse carcass.

Chapter Two

First Taste of the City

For our senior trip, instead of going to Sacramento, as we always had, we went to San Francisco because some other students and I talked Principal Horowitz into letting the student council decide where the trip went. As a member of the student council, I lobbied hard for San Francisco. Mr. Horowitz called the president of State and asked him to recommend someone who could lead the trip to make sure we wouldn't be led astray. President Olson suggested he use a man named Estaban Ortega, and as it turned out, I couldn't have been more pleased.

As soon as everyone was seated in the charter bus, Estaban introduced himself. "I'm thrilled to be leading your senior trip. This marks the beginning of your lives as adults, and I urge you to fulfill your destiny and make sure you make time to enjoy it. Do not shy away from it. A little bit about me. You saw my plastic name tag, so you know my name is Estaban. I am a graduate student in San Francisco State's human psychology department, and my thesis is gay men's influence in the formation of San Francisco. I came out last week as a proud gay man to my mom and dad. I share an apartment with my

friend Bill in what we call the 'Swish Alps' in San Francisco."
He winked at me as if I knew what Swish Alps meant, but I
did not.

The bus pulled onto the Golden Gate Bridge, and Estaban,
standing behind the driver with a hand on his seat for stability
and a skinny silver microphone in his other hand, began his
talk. "San Francisco is a federation of tribes that didn't feel
welcome where they started, be it Tegucigalpa, Honduras, or
Bridgeport, Connecticut, where I grew up." I couldn't stop
staring at the bulge in his pants.

As we drove along the waterfront, Estaban took the mic
again. "I ran away from home to come here, and folks like me
have been doing that since the first ships brought people to
these wharfs from New York and New Orleans in 1848. Many
of the crews deserted their ships, leaving hulls in the muck
of beautiful San Francisco Bay over there. Some stayed and
others took off for the gold fields and both left a richer gene
pool in Northern California." Further down the waterfront,
Estaban said, "After serving in Korea, my cousin Frankie, who'd
disembarked in Oakland, met Oscar, who'd also disembarked
at the Black Cat, an open-to-all bar on the waterfront. He
decided it was better to stay with Oscar in San Francisco than
live alone in his parents' basement in Quincy, Illinois."

I laughed and that got the others laughing.

George Stubbins, with thick glasses, who did better than
me in math classes, raised his hand. Estaban allowed him to
speak.

George said, "The city was founded by rough seamen, so I
don't see how they could be gay unless they were the commies
involved in the early Russian fur trade."

"George, do you know any gay men?" Estaban said,
stifling his laughter at George's ignorance about gay people
and Russian history.

"No, I don't, sir, but I read a lot of history, so I know if
it weren't for San Francisco being a great port, it wouldn't be
much of a city."

"Maybe some of the rest of you also don't know a gay person, but we are just like you. The only difference is we are attracted to our own kind," Estaban explained.

One of the girls who called me uppity surprised me when she said, "My uncle's a homo and he looks like his brother."

"Once my thesis is printed I can make a copy available to any of you who are interested in how gay men helped shape San Francisco, but we need to keep on with the tour."

Two of the toughest kids in class grumbled, but several kids shouted, "I want one! I want one!"

A mean-looking girl in a school uniform across the aisle gasped, offended, but Estaban ignored her. As we passed Union Station, he continued, "When the transcontinental railroad was completed in 1869, it still took 83 hours to get from New York to San Francisco. Can you imagine it taking that long? The queer people on those trains could have been students, members of the armed forces, and opportunists in high-button collars."

A boy in back giggled at high-button collars, and the agitated girl started to get up. But the sweet-looking girl next to her, also in a school uniform, kept her back.

Estaban continued as we passed the Palace Hotel. "After two days in coaches without air conditioning, everyone wanted to change clothes, take showers, some took them toge..." He stopped, looking embarrassed, and avoided looking at me.

Passing through the gates of Chinatown, Estaban started up again. "I think of every neighborhood here as a side show. The hawkers for the sideshow are the things and people that try to lure us in, like the small Chinese man who handed me a menu at the door of that restaurant over there. There's also the smell of grease and cilantro in the Mission, which we will see next, that induced me to ask the server in the Mexican restaurant to spoon a portion of carne asado onto my plate. Now, imagine the pierogi in the window of the Russian bakery in the Richmond. In case you don't know, a pierogi is a meat-filled pie. We're coming up on the Richmond later so close your eyes and imagine that pierogi talking the baker into sliding it between sheets of wax paper so we could take it home." Two girls giggled at the thought of a pierogi talking, poking each other.

The trip was silent for a while, with everyone staring out the windows at the passing scenery, but when the bus turned the corner at Market Street and headed down Castro Street, Estaban explained, excited, "There wasn't enough room on these sidewalks for all of us who were coming out when I got here. Coming out is a term that means we accepted our sexuality. We could be anyone we wanted to be. See all the second-hand stores? It's store's like that where I found the coolest furniture that didn't cost much when we furnished our first apartment. This neighborhood now has more gay men and lesbians than any other neighborhood in the city. Have you ever thought about that? How we tend to live near people like us?" The agitated girl, her face now red, started to say something and stopped when Estaban, with his hands on his hips, stared her down. He composed himself and went on. "I lived in a bell jar since the day I was born. From inside I could see what was going on around me, but I couldn't get there. I pushed against the side, but I couldn't pick up the peach. I tried to pry it from the bottom so I could kiss a boy, but it held steady. I was shocked that a place like San Francisco existed because it broke every rule in the book, but no one's stopped it yet!" The kid who read the most books in class cheered the city's accomplishment.

The bus pulled up to where we started and I broke out clapping. Most of the others, except the angry girl, with their heads down, looked like they were letting what Estaban said sink in. A few clapped.

Before we disembarked, Estaban had a final request. "I would like to ask you what you thought of the tour."

The toughest-looking boy in class clenched his fist. "You're gonna get arrested saying shit like that. I'm not one of you. I'm no homo because I work on my dad's cars. I don't really work on them but I help him. I never think of boys that way."

The agitated girl, her face still flushed, pointed her finger accusingly. "You are a terrible human being. You wouldn't believe how many friends I have, more than any girl, and I'm going to tell every single one of them that they should never, ever talk to you, much less look at you. You'll see." She started crying and her friend held her.

Two boys who were good at sports, whose names I never remembered, looked at each other, nodding at a shared secret. When I got off, I tugged Estaban's sleeve. "Thank you."

As I walked to my bike, I heard Estaban behind me talking calmly to the agitated girl, who'd stopped crying.

A couple weeks later, my next-door neighbor, Mrs. Kowalczyk, whose girth suggested that her appetite for the cabbage-wrapped balls of ground meat, onions, and carrots she brought to the house every time I was sick, was as huge as her appetite for the juiciest gossip, whispered to me confidentially in her kitchen, "The parents of one of the girls who was on that senior trip of yours are so angry at the way she was treated that they got the parents of all the other children on the trip to sign a letter to the president of State, demanding that he suspend that sick man who led the tour."

I said nothing.

"You're a sweet young man, and I can tell you tried to get off the bus, but that sick man made you stay. I've been saying State is a hotbed of red commies and their ilk. Education should be teaching kids to be decent, law-abiding citizens, not the drugged-out delinquents that State's turning out."

I hid my smile. "Is that another of your pork roasts I smell?"

The men and boys in Point Reyes Station cowered when I even alluded to their dicks, but in San Francisco, I would let mine hang so it could be seen. Small, big, medium won't matter. It's my dick and I'm proud of it.

Chapter Three

Christopher Robin

I was seventeen and was starting to get some meat on my scrawny frame. I'd ridden a scooter that cost a pretty penny on Pops' tight budget to the lighthouse at Tomales Point. The wind washed over me as I read my copy of *Huckleberry Finn* to prepare myself for running away. It was rare to see anyone there, but I heard footsteps getting closer. They weren't the stiff steps of boots, more likely sandals. A voice behind me asked me why I was there. I told the man, "I'm reading this little bible." He thought that was a funny way of saying it, but he wasn't trying to embarrass me the way the men on the docks did when I said things like that. I asked him what he was doing there, and he said, "You always find men like us at the end of land. This lighthouse could be the one in Key West or the one in Provincetown."

I didn't know what that meant, but it intrigued me, so I turned to an older man my height with a strong nose, a high forehead, and short, tightly-curled chestnut hair. His lips were thin but they were smiling. That was the beginning of the strangest day.

The way his eyes darted suggested he was exceptionally intelligent, and I thought he could be one of the special men that I imagined lived in big cities like New York and London with other men like them. They had secret handshakes and passwords and met at secret hideaways wearing berets and smoking reefers. I also imagined that they did illegal and immoral things to each other, which made them more seductive. Were those men real, and could I actually be talking with one of them?

"What is your name?" I asked. A gull swooped for a fish in the bay behind me and missed.

"I'm Christopher Robin, and my address is Pooh Corner."

"What's your real name?" I was sure he was one of the secret men.

"Names are bait, and you shouldn't get hooked on something that isn't who I am." His voice had a singsong quality I found attractive.

"Are you embarrassed about your name?" I asked him, wanting his answer to reveal his membership in that secret life.

"Are you embarrassed about being gay?"

"Embarrassed about being gay? That's ridiculous." I was sure he was one of them, but I was afraid he wouldn't consider me good enough to be granted entry into his secret society, so I was defensive.

"Have you told your parents?" The gull tried a second time and this time it was successful.

"I don't have to tell you." Now I wasn't sure he was one of them, and I had to protect myself.

He sat on a rock and patted the space next to him. "Let's talk, 'cause I think you know who you are."

I was caught off-guard and scrambled to come up with something to say. I finally asked him, "Who are your friends?"

"I probably have more than you have."

"Ollie's my friend." As soon as I said it, I thought I should have lied and said I had tons of friends.

"Every man should have a friend for each of his moods, so when you're up, you have a friend to do things with. When you're down, there's another friend who listens to you."

"If you have so many friends, where are they?"

"Don't be a smart-ass! I'm not going to bite."

"Where are they?" I wanted friends like that.

"They're keeping me alive." He swirled his hand around his head to suggest that's where his friends were.

"Where the fuck are they?" I shouldn't have cussed, but I had to know for sure.

"Up here," he said, pointing to his head.

"Those can't be real friends." I thought maybe he was using a code language that I didn't understand.

"Look, kid, my life is shit and it has been for years, but I wasn't going to spend the rest of it like my tight-ass brother. When you're different, you make up your friends."

"So, your friends are imaginary." I liked the idea and hoped he'd tell me how I could make imaginary friends who seemed as real to him as his.

"They're just as real as ol' Huck Finn."

"But they can't hold you." I didn't know where that came from, and I tried to backtrack. "But that doesn't mean I want you to hold me."

He thought for a minute. "What if I held you?"

I felt he was looking through me, so to stop it, I closed my eyes and turned away. Random thoughts collided; I didn't know where they were coming from or where they were going. I tried to catch one before it ran into another and it dissolved. I was so rattled I had to get away from him.

Frustrated and angry, I got up, dusted off my pants, and stomped off. I ended up in the shade of some spurge brush. As I sat there, I remembered seeing Ollie in the shower and feeling something. I wasn't sure what the feeling was, but I wanted him to be more than just a friend. Then I was suddenly possessive and Ollie could only be my friend. I asked myself, "Does that make me a homo?" I wasn't a bad person; I never hurt anyone. The two ideas, bad homo and nice me, stuck together like bricks and mortar, and I couldn't pry them apart. I couldn't see either of them clearly, so I picked up stones and threw them as hard as I could at the roots of the nearby brush. Each missed and glanced off into the gnarly underbrush landing in distant sand. After several failed attempts, my anger was raging. A tree root became the victim of my rage, and I stomped on it with all my force until it was nothing more than strands of pulp in the sand. I turned to leave but when I took a step, my foot screamed with pain because the stomping had made a hole in the sole of my shoe. When I stepped on a sharp rock beneath the hole, it slashed my foot, sending searing pain up my leg. "Fuck!" I fell to the ground screaming nonsense.

I heard him approaching and scooted into denser shade, hoping he wouldn't see me. I waited, listening, and minutes later I heard him sit on the other side of the brush and ask over the sound of the wind if I'd read Robert Frost. I said didn't know him, and he said he was a poet who wrote about paths in the woods, and I should be careful to choose the path less traveled. If he could have seen my face, he would have known I never followed the crowd, so I told him, "The kids at school are gonna spend the rest of their lives here, but I'm gonna cross the Golden Gate Bridge."

"Sorry, kid, this is just a stop on my way to a meditation center in England, and I have to get back into town to catch a bus."

"But what about me?" What the fuck?

"Tim Park lives in San Francisco. I'm going to write his name and phone number of this scrap of paper." He scribbled a number on it and handed it to me. "I should get going before it's dark." He disappeared as quickly as he appeared.

I'd seen my fair share of weirdos in the café, but none of them had seen something in me as he did. I didn't know what I expected to find in San Francisco, but I knew I'd be leaping into a big unknown. I admitted that I was indeed a homo. If I crossed the bridge with nothing more than a crumpled phone number, I could end up on the street. The negatives spun out of control, but a low rumble insisted that I had to cross the bridge.

Chapter Four

Never Stop Believing

1971

I couldn't get San Francisco out of my mind; the thoughts came back unannounced. After weeks of swaying back and forth between staying and leaving, I knew I was strong enough to cross the bridge. I had to be a man and not sneak out in the middle of the night, so I stood proud on the concrete block that served as our porch with a duffel bag with my earthly possessions. Pops was in the shadow of the portal, and I stuck out my hand. He didn't move. All I saw was the pulsing veins in his neck. He said nothing, so I turned to leave. He went inside and closed the door firmly.

I was in the clouds as the Greyhound Scenicruiser passed the long grasses of Sonoma County fields with grazing Holsteins. I was imagining what I was going to do in San Francisco when the fields gave way to the steep hills of Marin, proudly guarding it from the Bay. I couldn't sit still when the low Bay marshlands, thick with canvasback, pintail, and mallard, passed beside me in a flash. My excitement was almost more than I could bear as we crested the final range and went out of the tunnel onto the bridge, nirvana's golden entrance to the Bay. Each time I passed beneath a tower, I pulsed. Once in the city, I slid the window open so I could inhale my future. Block after block of beautiful Victorian homes flew past so fast I couldn't see them, but I wanted to go back and look at them slowly and find the one I wanted to live in.

By the time the bus pulled into the terminal, I was jazzed with bravado masking my fear. I pulled my bag from the overhead rack, almost crushing an elderly Asian woman who was waiting until everyone had gotten off before exiting. I apologized profusely and stepped onto asphalt unable to control my mind as it whirled with sunny shafts of possibilities. With my duffel stowed for a quarter, I scurried along a street littered with trash and the occasional needle. A dark-haired woman in a low-cut dress with tangerine lipstick stood outside a bar. Homeless men in threadbare suits that they probably bought for their weddings the day they returned from serving in Korea were good and drunk. They were waddling arm and arm up the sidewalk towards me. I avoided looking but their odor lingered long after they passed me.

I got in line for the cable car. When it was my turn, I hopped aboard along with a gang of under-dressed tourists talking over each other as they tried to stay warm. A hard, plastic handhold kept me balanced as the car jerked up Powell Street. Every time the black conductor in his neat gray uniform and cap clanged the bell, a man with straight red hair cut in bangs next to me nudged me with his hip. Did he mean what I thought he meant? My pants responded.

He got off halfway up the hill, and he signaled me to join him. Astonished by his interest, I wasn't sure what was going to happen, but I went along. I was greeted by his giggling friends who were more alive than the boys I grew up with; they all had mustaches and one had a beard. They talked gleefully around me as we walked up the block and climbed a wide staircase to an apartment on the second floor of a once-grand brick apartment building on the side of Nob Hill. A Janis Joplin at the Fillmore Auditorium poster ripped off a wall had pride of place in the main room. The windows were bare, and an Indian bedspread served as the door to the kitchen. Looking at each other, brimming with excitement, they began peeling off their clothes and adoring each other's body. I froze. The redhead, Rusty, put his arm around my shoulder to let me know nothing bad was going to happen, but it was hard to believe that I who had just gotten off the bus from Point Reyes Station had something that these men wanted. He broke the ice by asking my sign, and once I'd identified as a Pisces, the rest of them treated me as one of them.

In clouds of happiness, the oldest and ruggedly handsome asked if I saw *Boys in the Band*. Before I could answer, the youngest, exuding happiness from every pore of his olive skin, interrupted saying he was excited about a book he'd just read that I had to read. He wrote the name down on my wrist so I wouldn't forget. Two dark-haired men with almost identical lanky bodies, whom I took to be lovers, asked if I'd eaten the stuffed pork chop at this restaurant or the deep-fried calamari at that one as if they were the Stations of the Cross. I blushed with embarrassment at my ignorance. I had finally disrobed, but I was shaking when a goofy-looking guy with big ears asked if I'd seen the Palace of Fine Arts. Before I could answer, a man with a beautiful mustache said he would take me there with a picnic lunch of "This cool pâté I just found and a bottle of bubbly." A blond surfer-looking man said he'd make both of us his southern fried chicken so there'd be plenty.

I nodded in agreement at what they said, but I didn't understand how they could be interested in a country kid. I wanted them to know how much I appreciated their interest and had to find a way of saying it respectfully. Before I could come up with something, they stood in a circle. From the way they looked at each other and me, I saw the bond that existed among gay men just because we are gay men. The way they welcomed me made me feel that I was on sacred ground and was honored to be alive in their presence. I stowed my clothes behind a couch, ready but unsure for whatever came next.

Seven of us naked men sat in a circle on a many-generations-used Oriental carpet. The goofy guy opened the tea tin between his legs and extracted a plastic bag of weed and a packet of papers. The beautiful man with the mustache took out a paper and expertly rolled a joint with the grass that Goofy funneled into his folded paper. The joint was ritually lit and passed around the group, and each inhale was treated as a sacrament. It was passed a second time more casually, and when it got back to where it started, the aroused lovers got up and headed to the back of the flat while I stared at their naked butts in shock. Where did they get the balls to expose their erections? Beautiful Mustache put a Pointer Sisters LP on the turntable, and their bouncy tune had me wiggling with the rest of them as wildly affirming feelings of being part of a family shot through me like gentle lightning. Rusty raised his brows in question, and before I knew what I'd done, I raised mine in agreement. This was going to be my first sex with a man, the pinnacle of all the nights when I lay in the dark, trying to imagine the unimaginable. Now it was happening.

When his moist lips pressed against mine, the most extraordinary feelings seized me. I didn't want it to stop. When he held me, I had what I had wished for my entire life, and my tongue slipped into his mouth as though designed to do so.

We'd been eating each other like sacred animals for a long stretch when he pushed back enough to get on his knees. I went to keep on eating him, but he pulled me up with both hands. With me trembling, we entered a long hall. Each step meant I was closer to engaging in the mystery of sex with a man. When we got to a dark bedroom, I was shaking so hard I was afraid he'd toss me aside. I was about to be anointed a gay San Franciscan in the incense-infused chamber. Wind chimes outside the window tinkled high, low, and middle tones in perfect harmony. Rusty wrapped me in his arms, and we plunged onto the waterbed. As we sloshed around, he got on top of me and our lips met. I wanted all of what had made him a man inside of me. With his breath in my ear, his warm chest on my back, his belly in the small of my back, and his pelvis over my ass, our energies exchanged. I fell through the looking glass.

I'd never felt anything so extraordinary, and I had to make animal love to him, unable to get enough of his lips, touch, and smell. Swells of ecstasy washed over me each more ecstatic than the last. As we played around on the waterbed, the kid from Point Reyes Station became a man!

Dripping wet and sizzling with amazement at what had just happened, I was blissfully exhausted as I merged with the gently moving pod of water. With his easy breathing next to me, I wondered what Pops would think of the smile on my face, one he'd never seen.

After a quick shower and thanking Rusty for the best time of my life, I devoured the thick bacon, hash browns, and eggs that Muscles made as he hummed "Over the Rainbow." While the others were eating, I took the scrap of paper from my pocket and flattened it so I could read it. The hugs as I went around the room were the warmest I'd ever felt. I went to hall, where someone left his bike, and called the number. The phone rang and rang, and just as I was about to put it down, sure that the number was a hoax, an annoyed voice answered, "How many times do I have to tell you, I'm not dying and not interested in loving care insurance!"

I told him my name and that someone who called himself Christopher Robin had given me his number.

He laughed. "What's he up to this time?" I told him he was on his way to a meditation center in England, and he laughed again. "You didn't take him seriously?"

"I thought he was one of the men who knew the secrets," I said.

"He's not quite right. I should explain. Would you mind dropping by?" He gave me his address and, holding the phone in the crook of my neck, I scribbled the address on the pad next to the phone.

On my way to Muni, I walked through the Civic Center,

where its magnificent domed City Hall, its matching pools, and colonnade of olive trees and its Beaux Arts buildings made me feel that this was a fairy tale kingdom. I knew it was my home. As I went up Market Street, the arms connecting the bus to the overhead power line bounced around, and I couldn't take my eyes off of them afraid that they'd slip off and the bus would crash. That would be the end of me in San Francisco.

I thanked the Universe that I was still in one piece when I got off the bus at the corner of 17th and Market. By the time I climbed the 17th Street hill and got to the midcentury apartment building, my armpits had made dark, musty rings in my one good shirt. Tim, sporting a blue sport coat, paisley cravat, and white pants, was waiting for me in the open ground-floor garage. "I'm so sorry you crossed paths with Thad. He's my brother, and he's been in and out of but let's get you upstairs so you can freshen up." I followed him up a metal and concrete slab open staircase in the courtyard to the third floor and across an open passageway with a view of the courtyard to his door. He swung it open and ushered me in. A narrow passageway separated a deep blue Air Wick-scented bathroom from a brilliant white kitchen, and the colorless living room at the end had sliding glass doors, and behind it was a jungle on the deck with an elephant ear plant, a potted palm, and a cross-legged table with succulents each set in fine china flea-market soup bowls.

"Don't be shy, the bedroom's over there. There's also a bath so you can shower, and oh, use the towel on the rack." The yellow bedroom with yellow swag drapes was daintier than I expected. His four-poster bed with stuffed giraffes at the head was not the masculine bed I expected.

Hot water beat a tattoo on my head. As I inhaled the steam, I gave myself credit for what I'd done. I hoped Tim would know somewhere near where I could see gay men in action. I came back with water spotting my jeans as Tim was about to light a thin cigarette as he reclined on an off-white sectional. "If you haven't already found something, I have a vacant apartment," he said without getting up. I told him it was my first day in town, so he grabbed his keys and walked me to the second floor and showed me a one-bedroom apartment with a balcony. It had sliding glass doors in the living room and an adjacent bedroom like his and the kitchen was tiny. I'd never had my own place and to me it was perfect. I thanked him for thinking of me. I was in heaven when I rented my first living room, bedroom, and kitchen.

When we got upstairs, I was about to ask him about a place I might see gay men in action, but he asked me if I wanted something to drink. I said I'd like sparking water. He returned with a gin and tonic.

"I asked for sparkling water."

"Sensible men drink hard liquor and the vodka was half gone."

"Who do you think I am?" I wanted him to be my champion.

"Dear, you have a lot to learn. The only civilized way men meet each other is over dinner and drinks in a private home. I know what you're going to say, and some men do get drunk, but at least they do it in the privacy of a home. These new bars are going to make things worse."

"Is there somewhere nearby where I can watch gay men?" Being corralled into a routine sent ice through my veins.

"The neighborhood is going to hell in a handbasket."

"I'd like to see a gay bar."

"Dear, they're all over the place, and you must be careful if a good-looking man offers to buy you a drink because you'll end up doing something you'll be ashamed of." He was my landlord so I told him that I'd be careful, but I almost fell when I raced down the steps.

Men dressed like the man that I'd had sex with stood outside Toad Hall, but I approached cautiously. A tall dark-haired man saw my hesitant face. "You look like you're new in town."

"I am."

"Let me be the first to welcome you to Oz. I still can't believe it's real."

I wanted to ask him about what it takes to be gay, but I didn't know how, so I stood there confused. I couldn't believe my luck when he said he grew up in Marshall, just up the coast from Point Reyes Station, so I knew I could trust him. I dragged him into the closest café so we could have a nice long conversation as he explained what it means to be a gay man.

We sat on bent metal-back chairs at a small table, and I cleared the crumbs with the plastic menu. "Can I buy you a coffee or whatever?"

With the smile of a beneficent uncle he said, "I'm fine, thanks, but you look like you're about to burst." A waiter as old as the café took my order and minutes later returned with it. I spread my napkin in my lap. "I have so many questions, but I'm so happy to be here I forgot to get your name. I'm Charlie."

"It's nice to meet you, Charlie. I'm Ken. You said you have a lot of questions so I'd be glad to answer. They are likely the ones I had, and I wish someone had been there for me."

"They probably are." I couldn't believe someone would do that for me.

Ken started by describing cruising, the way men signal their interest in another man. He said to use my eyes to let him know I'm interested. If I get a positive response, I can approach him. That was going to be a challenge because I had a hard time looking at a man, much less his eyes. He explained that most men met each other in bars. The bars closed at 2 AM. After that was last call, when men who hadn't made a date stood outside the bar or in the nearby park. When I asked him how often he had sex, he said, "I have sex every day, and I just came from a playdate with a man I met last night in a bar." My mind went crazy as I tried to calculate out how anyone would have the energy to do that, but then, my experience with sex was limited and maybe having sext gave you energy. I asked how could there be that many men to have sex with. He said a professor friend at San Francisco State told him that 1,000 gay men a month came last year, so I wasn't alone, but the number was staggering. I didn't have the slightest idea what I would do if a man came home with me to have sex, so I boldly asked if he would tell me what he does on a date. He laughed saying of course he would, so I asked how he started a date. He said, "I spend an hour or two before he gets there. I clean the apartment and put a moving pad on top of my bed and make sure I have a ready supply of lube and poppers."

"What are lube and poppers?" I asked. He went into the details about different kinds of lubes and the difference between cheap and expensive poppers, but what impressed me was his thoroughness; he took sex seriously.

When he said he'd had anal sex, that sounded dirty. I checked his face to make sure he was telling the truth. To comfort me he said, "You needn't stick to one kind of sex because there's also cocksucking and frottage." Anal piqued my interest because the thought disgusted me.

"Nothing compares to the feeling of having a man inside me. They invented the word bliss for that feeling."

I shifted to hide my erection.

He went on, assuming I'd like anal sex, about using a douche hose to clean my ass. That set me back. Shitholes were for shit and having water inside my ass would mean constant diarrhea. He insisted that unless my ass was clean, I couldn't enjoy anal sex. "You flush your ass with water, you don't store it there so it's spic and span when you play."

He kept checking my responses to see if I liked what he said about anal sex. He must have seen my erection because he smirked. My mind was tumbling, but I built up as much courage as I could. I crossed a line and asked him, "Why don't you want me?"

"I like younger guys," he said as if he was being nice to them by having sex with them.

"But it sounds like you're doing them a favor." The donut I dunked in my tea dissolved before I could pull it out.

"Sex is something we have to do. I'm sorry I've been sounding like your mother."

"No, I just got here. Are there other places I could see men being gay?"

"I'm thirty and over the hill. The boys in the bar I went to didn't see me," he said, laughing to himself at my ignorance.

"You're not that old."

"You have much to learn," he said, resigned.

I looked at my reflection in an empty glass and tweaked a lock of hair. "Is there any alley where I could have sex?"

"You're young and your testosterone is flowing like a mighty river. You might as well end up in a gay bar. If I were you, I'd go to Toad Hall. That, I'm told, is pretty safe."

"I can't thank you enough."

"It's getting late." He started to get up.

"No, please, one more, Ken?" I had to see gay men in action.

"Actually, you could go to the baths, that might be easier."

"The baths?"

"Baths are places men have sex. I know what you're thinking, but there actually are such things. They have cubicles where the men have sex."

Coins were shaking in my pocket as I stood in line at Ritch Street Baths. The lobby glowed red, and a cute man behind the glass after I paid him five dollars passed me a towel and a key on an elastic loop with a plastic coin with the number 78. He pointed to a door. I went through the door and followed a man in a towel until he got to a locker room, where I left him and found locker 78 that was hard to see in the dark. I got undressed thinking about how I had sex with the men my first day in town to prepare me.

I walked around both floors of cubicles in a daze. A few were empty, some had the door closed, and I heard men having sex in most of them. One had a not particularly good-looking man lying next to a phalanx of dildos, and I didn't have to be told what they were used for.

I met a nice man my age named Ryan Southland in the little café. We spent an hour having sex in one of the cubicles.

Over the next weeks, I made dates every night. Each time it was easier. The men I played with cared for me and wanted to know more about me. They also went out of their way to make me feel at home.

Once I'd proven to myself that I could hold my own, I began the happiest years of my life.

Chapter Five

"There's no love like the first."
—Nicolas Sparks, novelist

My first crush was on the man who lived across the hall from me in Tim's building. His dark brown hair had streaks of silver, and I thought he was a god. I immediately liked the way he carried himself the first time I saw him walking down to the garage. He always left his apartment at 7:45 AM with a paper bag that I assumed was his lunch, but he looked like he could afford to go out to lunch. He wore tailored suits and he had a collection of colorful ties that perfectly matched his shirt and the suit he was wearing that day. I knew diddly about style or fashion labels, but to naïve me, he epitomized an executive. For someone who grew up in a little town of rough men, he made a big impression. There was something kindly about him, and I thought whatever he did, he did it to make life better for someone. I opened the door just a crack, so he couldn't see me, but after he passed, I went to the bedroom and jacked off with his smoldering hazel eyes on the screen in my mind. I didn't want Tim to think I was a sneak, so I never asked him who he was. I think part of that was that I wanted to keep him my secret.

He surprised the hell out of me when he stopped me one

night as I was racing out to a date that I was already late for. I didn't want the man who'd invited me to be pissed. Ellery was someone I traded cruises with every time we saw each other in a bar, but neither of us had ever stopped long enough to say something. When he did last night, he caught me off-guard, and of course I said yes. So if I showed up at his apartment on Eureka Street late for our date, he'd think I was just a quick fuck.

"I've seen you watching me," the man said.

"I didn't want you to think I'm a sneak," I said.

"When a door's open a crack, there's a good chance someone is trying not to be seen."

"I'm sorry. I didn't think you could see me."

"I noticed your pants were wet when you came back the other day. What do you do?" He eyed me up and down.

"I'm the go-to guy for a photographer. I keep the chemicals properly stored, that kind of thing." Even though the pair that I was wearing was dry, I covered them, embarrassed.

"Are you a photographer?" he asked. I noticed in the light that there were flecks of gold in his eyes that made him even more appealing.

"I can't afford it," I admitted.

"The Y has free classes and they loan you cameras."

"I didn't know that." I didn't think that I had it in me to become a professional photographer, although I often wondered what the photographer who took the photos of men in posing straps like the ones I saw in *Physique Pictorial* looked like. Was he as good-looking as his models or a dirty old man?

"Would you do me a favor?" he asked.

"Sure." His smile was hard to resist.

"Hold on." He slipped into his apartment and came back with a book wrapped in brown paper tied with string.

"Will you take this to a friend?" he asked.

"OK, I guess. Does he live around here?"

"Here's his address. All you have to do is give him the book and make sure he sees you." He put the book with the address in my hand.

"Shouldn't I say something?" I asked, unsure of what he was asking me to do.

"No. You'll be fine. Off you go." He went back into his apartment and closed the door.

That was not what I wanted to hear, but I didn't want to disappoint him, so that afternoon, I got on Muni and headed for North Beach. The bus took me as far as Stockton Street, so I had to walk through Chinatown. The smells coming out of the restaurants that I passed on my first time in Chinatown made me want to stop and sample all of the dishes until I got to a restaurant that had colored photographs of its dishes on display in a lit case next to the entrance of the restaurant. When I saw chicken's feet and another that looked like worms, I wasn't so sure about sampling the food in Chinatown without a guide.

I'd never been in North Beach, and I loved walking Grant Avenue with thoughts of Allen Ginsberg walking where I was walking in what I imagined Italy looked like with red and green banners and a lot of foot traffic. Old men talked animatedly over tiny cups of espresso under an umbrella outside a café, and a large family squabbled loudly and lovingly around a large round table in another restaurant that was open to the street, where the aromas of oregano and red sauce filled the air. I envied them for living in such a large family. They seemed to be happy with each other and spending time together. That is what I always wanted but never had with Pops after Mom died. Our dinners were mostly him talking about something that happened in the Bay, like the sick sea lion, and his meals were mostly canned food and warmed-up frozen French fries. If I hadn't moved to San Francisco, where I had buddies that were my family, I thought I would have ended up like the kids I grew up with, stunted and dull.

I found the address, a handsome two-story wood Victorian tucked between similar stucco buildings on a narrow steep side street. I was out of breath when I got to his address, so I stopped and calmed down enough to look my best when I knocked on the door. A tall, good-looking man in a deep red smoking jacket opened the door. "What do you want?" He looked me over." You sure you have the right address?"

"I was told to give you this." I handed him the book wrapped in brown paper tied with string.

"What the hell is this?" he said as he looked the book over and turned it around.

"He didn't tell me."

"He didn't' tell you? Who is he? You must know who gave it to you." He sounded suspicious.

"It was the handsome man who lives in my building."

"I'm sure he's very nice, but what is his name?" His tone softened.

"I never asked. He lives across the hall." He was trying to coax it out of me, but I'd made a horrible mistake by not asking the man across the hall his name.

"You don't know his name? That's not very nice if he's your neighbor," he said cynically.

"Sorry, I never asked him, but I see him all the time." I could tell he was getting angry, and I was pissed that I never bothered to ask the man his name. What a stupid thing to do! It's not that hard, I could have asked him his name but I didn't. Now I was making a fool of myself. I guessed I was too impressed with his good looks to ask him his name.

"Would you turn around?"

I turned around so I couldn't see the look on his face as he sized me up. As I turned, I flattened my shirt in case it looked too wrinkled.

"What do you do, young man?"

"I assist a photographer."

He was silent for a minute and then he said with sadness, "Please take this back."

"But he said I should give it to you and I didn't have to say anything." Over his shoulder, I saw that all the artwork in his apartment was covered with pieces of black fabric like pieces torn from sheets.

"I suggest you take it back to whoever told you to give it to me." He refused to take it and turned around.

"But—"

He slammed the door shut and I heard him crying on the other side.

I'd never been so humiliated. Someone I'd thought was a decent person sent me on a wild goose chase and I'd hurt someone. I was pissed as hell that I never asked him what I was taking or about the person I was to give it to. I shouldn't have been intimated by good-looking men, damn it! I'm a perfectly decent person.

Riding back on Muni, I didn't see the point in someone delivering a package to someone who doesn't want it. I wasn't sure what I was going to say to Tim. I was too embarrassed to talk about it when I got back, so it simmered inside me for days. I thought I was a rational person, but no matter how I tried to come up with a rational explanation for why the man whose name I forgot to ask did what he did, I had failed.

Then it dawned on me. I had long suspected that good-looking people lived in a special world of their own, where they associated with each other. I heard about this place called Newport, Rhode Island, where East Coast barons like Vanderbilt built huge homes next to the sea. I supposed that's where those people went in America. But they also lived in San Francisco, because he was one of them. Some of the younger men of that kind ventured into gay bars because one afternoon when I was in Sutter's Mill, a gay bar in the Financial District, I overheard two men in elegant suits talking about the sport coats from Wilkes Bashford, a high-end men's clothing store, that they wore when they took a personal jet to Puerto Vallarta. "Mine was simply divine. His home was decorated down to the door hinges."

I suspected the man who lived in my building was one of them, too, although I never saw him in a gay bar, so I didn't know if he was gay. He and the man that didn't take the package were playing games on me. They were using me, a kid from a small town, as the subject for their ridicule; they were using me to prove to each other that they were superior to everyone.

That made me feel worse and very small. I mentally flogged myself for getting caught in their game.

After a week of going out only for work and coming straight back and not going to the bars as I usually did because I was embarrassed to be seen in public, I'd had enough. I went to Tim's one night after dinner.

He was arranging a loose bunch of sunflowers in a vase that was too small for them, and there was water all over the counter along with shreds of sunflower. "Can I ask you something?"

"What's on your mind?" He took them out of the vase and started cutting the stems with a pair of kitchen scissors that didn't cut the stems and jammed. "Christ!" he muttered.

"You know that man who lives across from me?"

"Thomas?" He put the scissors down and found a knife in a counter drawer.

"Does he have silver streaks in his hair?" I asked.

"Does that bother you? He's a nice guy."

"That's what I thought, but he asked me to do something and either I screwed it up or he played a sick trick on me."

"He's not the kind to plays tricks." He smashed the stems with the handle of the knife, but they didn't get any shorter. "Damn you!" he yelled.

"I don't know if he wants me to tell you, but he asked me to take what looked like a book to someone who lives in North Beach, but he didn't take it."

"That's not like him. Why don't we talk to him?" He jammed the stems into the vase breaking half of them. "Shit!" He tossed them aside.

"He's going to hate me." I turned to leave.

"Thomas is the sweetest guy, and I'm sure he can clear it up."

"But I wasn't able to do what he asked me to do." The last thing I wanted was to face Thomas.

"Let's find out." He grabbed my arm and hauled me resisting down to the second floor. I stood quaking outside

Thomas's door. Tim rapped gently and seconds later Thomas opened the door. When he saw me, he pulled me into the warmest hug. "You did it, kid!"

"But I couldn't get him to take that package you gave me," I stuttered, stupefied and trying to free myself.

"The shrouds are gone. It was so good to see that," he said excitedly.

"I swear I didn't touch anything. I didn't even get inside his apartment so I wasn't near any of his art. I didn't want to hurt him." Thomas sounded like he thought I did something right, but I couldn't figure out what I'd done right.

"Let me explain. Philip lost his lover, Crawford Barton, who was a great photographer, six months ago. After he died, he covered all of Crawford's photos."

"I swear I didn't touch anything."

"Charlie, you're so full of life I knew that when Clarence saw you, he'd be reminded there were still men like the ones that Crawford loved taking photos of," Thomas explained.

"Why did you put me through all that crap? I think he was even crying at the end." I was still trying to get my head around what he said.

"I'm sure they were tears of joy," Tim corrected.

"But what about the package?"

"I'm sorry. I just needed a reason to get you somewhere he could see you."

"You should have explained before you sent me off on that stupid errand."

"I suspect he adores you," Thomas assured me.

"I'm sure he does," Tim confirmed.

"That doesn't make me feel any better." I felt that I'd been had.

Tim asked me to walk him back to his apartment and along the way he said, "I'm invisible, so no one notices me, but there's something about you that's very attractive. It's more than your looks. You have to find a way of dealing with people noticing you and wanting to be your friend because a lot of them will want to. Some do it nice and some don't."

"Bullshit!"

"Be serious. I don't say this because I'm jealous of your charm, although I wish I had some of it. But the reality is that you are going to get a lot of attention. That lesson wasn't the reason I had you to go, but it turns out to be a good lesson because everyone's going to want to know you. I can't protect you, but you're smart and I think you'll find a way of handling the attention you're going to get."

"You really think I'm that special?" I didn't have a very high regard for myself.

"You are to me and will be to a lot of other men." He kissed my forehead before going into his apartment and closing the door. "Sleep tight," he called from the other side.

Chapter Six

Twins

I met Tom and Ted Braithwaite on a hot summer day as fog tumbled slowly over Twin Peaks, waiting for it to flood the city. They were identical twins, and they were wearing matching tan Carhartts, blouse-like white shirts, and laughing at a joke one of them made in front a macramé artist's stand at my first Castro Street Fair. Without saying a word, they must have liked what they saw because they introduced themselves by jokingly sticking their fingers in my ears, which sent bolts across my brain. I stood five foot eleven, and they were a tad taller. Their torsos were long, their postures were that of Greek bronzes, and their builds evidenced manual labor. We discovered in quick chitchat that we shared the same birthday. With all of us being Pisces, they invited me to spend a weekend at their home on the Russian River. I'd heard stories about the good times men had at the river, so I was excited to see it. But even if they said they lived in Alameda, I would have jumped at the chance to spend the weekend with them because they exuded positive energy. I had tasted that kind of energy and wanted more.

They picked me up in their green Volvo station wagon. As Tom drove us out of town, I felt like an honored guest as Ted and I fooled around the back seat with their dog Tiger, a long-haired terrier. We drove up Highway 101 and Tom took the Sebastopol exit in Sonoma County, heading straight for the farmer's market on the square in the center of town. Ted wasted no time finding the bent-over man with a darkly tanned face in front of a trestle table of potatoes in various sized wooden boxes. I grew up on frozen French fries, so I didn't know there were various varieties of potato. He examined each like a caring parent, selecting just the right sized little red potatoes and the plumpest Yukon gold potatoes that he dropped into a paper bag. Tom, who'd wandered off, returned with a retro lamp under his arm. "It's a perfect match to the DeSoto hood ornament."

"Is that from the hot guy's stand?" Ted's eyes were hopeful.

"He's still straight," he said, grinning.

"You sure? He'd be so much fun."

The Russian River road that paralleled the river was one of the most beautiful drives I'd ever been on. Willows grew out of the river in the low parts. The beaches had potbellied dads with coolers, kids with plastic rakes, and clusters of chatting mothers. I kept looking for the hot men I'd heard about. When I asked when I'd be seeing them, Ted explained that we'd passed the turn off to the gay section at Wohler Bridge, I would see it tomorrow. Like so many of the men I'd met in San Francisco, the twins connected food with sex. They must have been attracted to the Bay Area because both were in abundance there. Ted talked about stuffing a turkey as if the turkey was a butthole and he said the skin of a peach was like a baby's bottom.

Tom said they had a nursery, but he acted as if talking about its success would be seen as being boastful. Instead he told me they grew peonies every year in their greenhouse, paying particular attention to the light and food so that they bloomed in December, well before they normally do. They could take bouquets of peonies to the home-bound elderly men in the county who didn't have families at Christmas.

"Each one of them also got a basket of jams we make from the fruit in our orchards."

That night, as the three of us lay beneath the stars with the river's muddy song in the distance, I felt their emotional warmth was wrapped around me like a warm pillow.

"Do you know about meditation?" Tom asked as I lay there.

"Yes, but I've never done it."

"Would you be interested?"

"Yes."

"We'll get a good night's rest so we'll be ready for it tomorrow. You sure you're ready? It takes patience."

"If you guys like it, I'm gonna like it." I would do anything for them.

We didn't get a good night's rest because once we got in bed, we started kissing. I was proud of being able to show the men on Nob Hill a good time one at a time. That made it easier for me to be comfortable with them, and they couldn't have made it easier. They let our play develop naturally. Once we started having sex, I found myself completely at ease. The evening was a gentle flow that moved from what felt like hours of massage to a luscious session of sucking dick, ending in sex. I can't remember the order that I played with them because in the dark, it was even harder to tell them apart, but what I remember is that they were both gentlemen who took sex seriously with a refreshing sense of humor. After climaxing twice over the course of the evening, I slept like a log beside them.

Tom made rice porridge for breakfast, which I'd never had. While the texture took a little getting used to, the overall taste was quite nice. Once we had finished and the dishes were done, Ted rolled out thin spongy yoga mats on the deck.

I thought I was flexible, but getting into the lotus position, I was awkward and I was sure I looked like a spastic.

"Close your mind. When something comes up, gently move it aside," Tom advised.

They sat in the lotus position effortlessly and with their eyes closed, they began chanting "Om," which at first annoyed me, but the sound methodically seduced me.

I gave up shutting down thoughts that kept blooming like fireworks and ended up on my side watching them. I didn't know where they went, but both of them seemed very far away. Their faces were perfectly smooth and they seemed at peace with the world.

Tom joked when they stopped, "You looked like a statue."

"I don't think I'll ever slow down enough."

We shared coming out stories throughout the afternoon. Theirs was growing up in a loving family with many siblings. Our stories were interrupted by Tom dashing into the house and returning minutes later with fresh fruit compote in hand-thrown bowls with warm shortbread fresh from the oven. I'd never eaten so well or felt so good while I was eating. Until then, a meal, especially when Pops was cooking, was shoving down necessities. When I think about it now, it was brutal. Tom and Ted treated each meal as a ceremony and each food item as a blessing.

I finished dinner way before either of them. They didn't say anything, but when I thought about it, I insulted them by not taking time to enjoy the meal they'd done so well for me. I hoped that I got back in their partial good graces when I said, "You guys are amazing with food."

"It takes a calm mind," Ted said as he cleared the dishes from the table.

"How did you learn how to cook?" I batted a mosquito about to have dinner on the blood in a vein in my neck.

"My grandparents had a bakery in Lewiston, and I learned everything in that kitchen. Grandma taught me to sense what I was making, to feel what I'm making as I make it," Ted said, washing the dishes.

"I learned it from the boss," Tom said, drying the dishes.

"But he's the better cook," Ted added, smiling.

That night after having sex, I fell asleep between them on

the deck like we were family. An exhilarating outdoor shower started the next day. They showed me how to use the douche hose, which wasn't as messy as I thought it would be. The feeling of being clean inside was remarkable, and Tom reminded me that "Anal cleansing is considered good for your body by health experts." Once again, another urban legend, that it was only gay men who fuck that douched, was debunked.

The half-naked men getting out of their cars with baskets and backpacks in the parking lot at Wohler Bridge confirmed the stories I'd heard about the men at the bars. They were just a taste for what was to come. We came fully prepared.

Once we got to the beach, Tom spread beach towels on a sloping part of the beach so we'd be in the shade, because at ten the temperature was already 92° F. The beach stretched as far as I could see. Along the shoreline, every square inch was occupied by sexy men in Speedos, some naturally fine torsos naked, and other naked men engrossed in habitat magazines. Tom covered me with coconut butter and when he finished, Ted reached from behind him and tapped the head of my penis saying, "Hello, little man!"

From time to time, one of them disappeared in the mounds of sands and brush behind the beach, coming back to report on what he'd found.

After swimming across the river and back, I dozed off on the beach and woke feeling like a 4th of July bratwurst on the hottest part of the grill. I dove back into the river and luxuriated in the undulating cool that swirled around me. Soaking wet with my skin on fire, I wandered into the undergrowth. I never cruised parks, so I didn't know what one does amidst the tangle of sandy roots and ice plants, so mostly I took in the spectacle of the loving brotherhood around me. On my way out, feeling that I'd put the Wohler Bridge bushes notch on my belt, an older man with chiseled features got down on his knees in the sand and proceeded to give me a very sweet blow job.

Shaking sand off his pecker, he introduced himself. "I'm Carlos."

I shook my hands dry and shook his saying, "Nice to meet you. This place is phenomenal."

"I call it 'God's Green Acre,' even though it's neither green nor an acre." He laughed as he protected his eyes from the sun.

That night Tom, Ted, and I sat around the fire pit on the deck next to a ring of towering redwoods, and they introduced me to Kahlil Gibran's *The Prophet*, which, as they read, mesmerized me. I quickly understood why they treated it with reverence. Tom passed a joint of grass they grew, and I put down my drink, took a hit, and I curled up next to Ted while Tom entwined his legs in Ted's. Throughout the evening, I floated stoned in the cool night air and the heat of the fire as their voices deep and reassuring read passages from *The Prophet*. They introduced me to a way of thinking and to a way of being in the world that was a stark contrast to the way Pops saw his world.

If I could put Pops' way in a nutshell, it would be something like Get as much as you can before some sonavabitch grabs it. His life was coarse and so was his philosophy of life, if you could call it a philosophy. I knew there was some of that in me and I was embarrassed that I thought that way. I liked to think I was a decent person, but I knew I wasn't; I could be cruel. Two passages of the book had me looking deep inside.

The first Tom read. "You talk when you cease to be at peace with your thoughts." I prided myself at being able to talk the tough guys out of beating the shit out of me. I talked to divert attention or to make a point at school, and I talked over Pops so I didn't hear his harangues, so that didn't make sense. I'd have to do some serious work if it ever was going to make sense.

Ted read the other passage just before we turned in. "Love one another, but make not a bond of love. Let it rather be a moving sea between the shores of your souls." When he finished reading, Ted wrapped Tom in his arms and kissed him lovingly. Knowing that I'd never been able to hold someone that way made me sad. I asked Ted to read it three times because it was that important to them.

"He gives us a different way of seeing things, and if you spend some time with his words, I think you'd see what he's talking about," Tom suggested.

"I'll give it a try." It was so important to them I knew there must be something in it that was just as important to me.

Thoughts of love without making a bond kept bothering me when I got back to the city. I felt unable to love. But if I could, I'd want to consume him. I'd want the steal all the parts of him that I admired and make them my own. Ted's final comment had been, "We work at being good people." Damn philosophy! Trying to make sense of it was so fucking frustrating yet I felt compelled to finally figure out what it meant to me. They also said if you love someone, you're supposed to let them go. What good is that? I was never good at making friends, but when Ollie was my friend I never thought of letting him go. If I had and he'd been smart, he'd have crossed the bridge, but the last I heard of Ollie he was working on a farm somewhere on the Mendocino coast."

I was looking for a used book of Michelangelo's sculptures that I'd seen in the main library. As I was wandering through a used book store, I spied a man with white beard in a threadbare suit and clean white shirt reading *The Prophet* in one of the alcoves, so I went out and bought copy. The twins treated Gibran's book as a holy book. Because I put a lot of faith in them, I knew if I read it over and over, I would eventually understand its meaning.

Chapter Seven

Company Town

In 1972, San Francisco was a company town and the company was gay bars. Strung like strings of lights, they were festivals of life and safe havens for those of us who came from homes that couldn't take our sexuality. I crossed the bridge to live, and I lived in the bars; they were my life-blood. Without them, I would have gotten poison ivy cruising Buena Vista Park. There were so many bars, I had no trouble finding a bar that fit my mood any day or one to match the kink that I wanted to explore. I stopped counting them at twenty-three because I'd never have time to see them all.

Growing up, I was the one asked last when selecting teams. When boys went out for football, I was in the library. I was called a brownnoser. But in a gay bar with my tribe surrounding me with similar stories, I felt the acceptance that I'd longed for as a kid. The men I met in the bars told me everything I needed to know about making a home; the various styles to choose from and the coolest places to buy furnishings that fit me and where to find great art that I could afford.

At first I thought the gay men who lived in San Francisco

knew the secret of being gay without shame, but I soon discovered that I had just as much aptitude and insight as the next man because all of us were figuring out how to live free after a lifetime of repression.

Cruising was a bare-knuckles way of making play dates, but in the new democracy, once I got the rhythm of cruising, substance mattered. With conventions constructed centuries ago stripped away, they revealed fascinating bits of their psyche as we were having sex.

Bars defined where I lived, the jobs I took, and my daily routine; I never lived more than ten minutes from a bar and only took jobs I could leave at five. I got up at seven, got to work at eight, left work at five, was in a bar by eight and in bed after having sex around one every day of the week for fifty-two weeks a year in my first years because I had a lot of men to meet and have sex with. All my friends were men that I met in bars and had sex with.

Everything I imagined what being gay would be like but never had in Point Reyes Station I found in a gay bar. The dark-haired bartender in the Midnight Sun was hotter than the star quarterback that I lusted after in high school. The easy-going bartender in Toad Hall was the confidant I never had back home. When I needed a friend to take on a picnic, I found him in a bar because the bars were the Harrods of gay, where I could find everything I craved, from sympathy over the loss of my dog from the ironic but caring Everett Lund to advice on coming out to my boss from Paul Merar, who came out to his boss at the Sierra Club. They also included sweet treats like coffee-colored Robert Scott whose kisses sent me into outer space, and lean cuts of meat like Rusty Dragon, who made love to me in a sling.

On any given night, the walls of any bar had some of America's finest men who like me were strangers in a new city making our first gay families. That sounds easy, but prejudice and fear had been drilled into us subconsciously by what we saw and heard around us every day as we were growing up. I got a hefty dose of it just living with Pops. Churches were built around scaring people away from what diverted them from concentrating on the church, like pleasure and taking care of oneself, but our priests were really each other. I could confess my "sin" of doing LSD to Steve Owsley.

When I began dating, Toad Hall was a regular stop because the easy vibe of flannel shirts and jeans was a non-threatening space where I developed my cruising skills. The men I met there, like Bob Corcoran, were decent put-together men who were fun to play with. Gregg Coates, with whom he shared a restored Victorian flat on Sharon Street, would sing along with me to Linda Ronstadt's *Heart Like a Wheel*. I was never disappointed by Toad Hall, but in a year, I changed and I started going to the Stud, which was then on Folsom Street. It was there Sam Skarda told me to be true to myself. "You are a beautiful person and don't let anyone tell you otherwise." Tom Smith told me to go for it. "Hells bells, the good stuff won't last forever and you're not going to die, so why waste precious time worrying?" Clay Grillo, the handsomest man in the bar, taught me how to get fucked. When camping on the Navarro River, he introduced me to the glory of psilocybin mushrooms. Much later I met Arti at the Rainbow Cattle Company and he showed me a new way of loving.

The bars were the center ring in San Francisco's circus, each carefully crafted to suit a particular neighborhood and a specific clientele. I bought platform shoes because everyone had them, but the only gay bar I'd be comfortable wearing them was in the Cinch on Polk Street also known as Polk Strasse. My new leather vest made its debut at the no-name bar on Folsom Street, named that because there was no sign on the bar. I met a wild man from the Upper Peninsula of Michigan in the Midnight Sun. Drake Viettelijä explained, "When the closest gay bar is a seven-hour drive, your fucking imagination gets you doing some crazy shit."

The bars were master classes in rejection that took many forms. I expected Kenny Daniels would go come home with me, but just as I was about to ask him, he had a sudden interest in someone on the other side of the room. Sanders Anderson used another excuse. "You're fascinating and I really want to know everything about you, but that would take an afternoon. Can I take a rain check?" Perfectly toned Ricardo's excuse was, "Barry kept telling me he and I should be boyfriends, but he never whispered I love you. I didn't feel he was being 100% present with me, so I cut it off." I preferred Peter Fisk's blunt "Fuck off." He didn't follow that with you asshole, so I knew he had his tastes and I had mine but we could still be friends.

The first time I was rejected, I was hurt because I'd done nothing wrong. I flogged myself for not being savvy enough to have the vocabulary that other men had that got men to go home with them. I bought a black leather jacket and practiced pickup lines, expecting to improve my chances of taking someone home, but by the fourth rejection, I had better things to do than feeling sorry for myself, because feeling sorry for myself hadn't made me feel any better.

The bars were fish bowls of differences. I wasn't attracted to twinks of any ethnicity, but if I had been, I would have found them in Club Rendezvous on Polk Street. When I wanted to know what life was like for black men, I spent an evening talking with black men in the Pendulum on 18th Street. I danced with some of happiest and sensuous Latino men in El Rio in the Mission. I wasn't much into drag, but when I needed a wig fix, I dropped by the Gangway in the Tenderloin.

Gay bars were not just the most interesting venues in town, they reminded me that we were a community of individual struggles as well as our common struggle to be accepted for who we were. Coming from a white, blue-collar town where my world was tiny, that made a big impression. I felt alone in Point Reyes Station, but I was like everyone else in a gay bar.

Every weekend, parties emptied by 11 because the men had left for the bars; it was more accurate than a watch. When men started putting on their coats, I knew it was close to 11. If I was caught up in a conversation and we talked past 11, there would just be the two of us talking in an empty apartment with the host silently emptying ashtrays, hoping we'd leave so he could get to the bars.

Pops was a lousy model and I operated with the limited protocol he drilled into me: respect your elders and never back down. I learned who I was by the way the men in the bars reacted to me. For the first time, I could be open in a bar. Because I felt safe when sharing my coming out story, I exposed things about me that I'd hidden so deeply that I forgotten they were there, like my love of beauty and my desire to be touched. The acceptance I got from men in the bars allowed me to see myself as the man I was. I didn't fret that I wasn't the man I should be or the man Pops expected. In a gay bar, I was a complete man with my own quirks. I couldn't imagine being able to do that anywhere else.

The men I met in the bars taught me how to treat other people, and they brought out nuances of feelings that I'd dismissed because they were hard to understand. When John Robinson described going all out to make his boyfriend's birthday a spectacular occasion, I beat myself up for not going out of my way to make Mom's birthdays special; I just got her a card at the shop where I got my school supplies. In civics class at John Muir High, I was taught to respect authority figures, but John Savage, one of the first out gay policemen I met at the Ambush, taught me to be skeptical of authority figures and not take everything they said as fact.

The bars also set the tone for the community like our church did back home. When I was new in town and needed a sense of the place, I asked a bartender. I heard about the airline crash from a bartender. I heard men organizing for a protest demonstration in a bar. The few public officials with guts enough to be seen with gay men and lesbians did it in a gay bar.

Bars were my source for men to have sex with. If the tenor of a bar was upbeat, I knew the man I met there that night would want to have as much fun as I did. If the tenor was off,

I'd have to be extra persuasive to get someone to come back to my place. Once there, I wasn't sure what shape he'd be in.

The bars during the day served as a community center. When I was down, their solitude served as a temporary mental health clinic.

Without its gay bars, San Francisco would have been just as much in demand as a tourist destination with lovingly preserved Victorian homes, an art deco bridge, and 19th-century cable cars.

Chapter Eight

New Man in Town

I met Daniel Chauncey, who called himself Danny, shortly after he moved to San Francisco. He was living in my first apartment in Tim's building. He was six foot 4 four and so skinny, Tim joked that he had to run around in the shower to get wet. We were sitting around the glass-topped coffee table in Tim's living room, where the only thing that had changed since the first day I saw it was a succulent brought in from the deck. The Castro Theatre sign in the distance had just lit up. Danny told me he came from a broken family in Eureka Springs, Arkansas; his mother was a devout Baptist who played "the role of Mary in the *Passion Play* that's put on every night during the summer months to adoring Christians at the base of the largest cross in the South, and my father worked on oil rigs and wasn't home much." Danny said Eureka Springs, once a Victorian spa popular with East Coast elites, was evenly divided between the Evangelicals who arrived by the busloads by the thousands every summer on one side of the valley, and on the other side was the original Victorian town that was the South's sole outpost for art freaks. "I sat at my friend Benjamin's feet as he built bird-like structures out of auto parts and came home smelling of motor oil."

"Is Benjamin gay?" I asked.

"He's straight, but his brother's gay. He brought me out."

"Were you lovers?"

"Nah, Leslie's a pansy. He ran around in dresses."

"Tell Charlie why you decided to come here." Tim handed him a vodka tonic.

"I got fed up with the cheap-shit gay bars. You have to drive all the way to Atlanta and then it's a bunch of sissies."

"So, you came here for—" I began to say.

"The men," he finished the query firmly.

"He said he's heard about Folsom Street, and I told him you were the man to talk to." Tim handed me a glass of Jack Daniel's neat.

Tim looked wan and malnourished, but I didn't say anything. I asked him, "Do you ever go out?"

"I'm too old for that. I don't even go to the baths anymore. I could just sit and watch, and there were some real teases."

"What are the baths?" Danny asked, his eyes full of questions.

"The baths refers to the bath houses in town where men go to have sex," Tim explained.

"Is it like a gym?" I could see the gears turning in his head.

"There are different kinds," I said, "but most have cubicles where men have sex. Some have big soaking pools and a couple of big fish tanks. The Hothouse just opened, and was designed for serious sex."

"What's serious sex?" Danny's questioning eyes made him look like an owl.

"How old are you and how long have you been out?" I inquired.

"I'm twenty and what does it matter how long I've been out?"

"When I describe serious sex, it scares some," I said.

"Shoot!" he said excitedly. Tim watched Danny's reaction apprehensively.

"For them it means fist fucking."

"You mean someone fucks with a fist?" He checked the room to make sure no one else could hear him.

"Some call it handballing," I said. Tim went to bar to make another round of drinks.

"I don't think I'm ready for that."

"That's why I wanted to get a feel for your experience. Fisting is an acquired taste, and you have to want to do it."

"What's Folsom Street like?" He finished his drink and put it on a coaster.

"There's the Eagle, the Leatherneck, My Place, and the Powerhouse. My favorite is the Stud."

"What am I supposed to wear?" He scanned me to see what I was wearing.

"Dear, you can spend a fortune on chaps and harnesses at Mr. S. and you can still go home alone," Tim said, regret plastered all over his face.

"Are jeans OK?"

"In some, anything's OK. I've seen men naked," I answered.

"Holy cow! What about others, 'cause all I brought are jeans." Tim had another vodka tonic in Danny's hand before he could finish the sentence.

"You passed them on the way here," Tim said.

"All of them were gay?"

"Around here there's my old favorite, Toad Hall, the Midnight Sun is up Castro Street, and Moby Dick is great if you want to be in the Castro but not in the center of things. The Pendulum's popular with black guys and there's a bunch more," I said.

"I liked the look of a guy who was in front of the one with the toadstool on the sign."

"That's Toad Hall."

"Be careful you don't fall in love with Michael," Tim advised like a pageant judge checking out entries.

"Does he hang there?"

"He's the bartender," I said and his pants paid attention to my answer.

"Can I talk to him?" He reached to tie his shoe and the elbow of his long skinny arm sent a succulent and a soup bowl flying.

"Sure," I said, smiling, interested to gauge his interest.

"But only when you order," Tim said angrily as he rushed to get a towel.

"Come on, Tim, he's the nicest guy in town."

"You pretty boys say that." Tim was mopping the floor and his back was to me.

"Tim talks about you all the time. Sorry I've monopolized the conversation, but I'd like to know why you came here," Danny said.

"He just knows the pretty ones," Tim interjected as he wrung out the towel.

"That could take the rest of the night. In short, there is no place like San Francisco. You can be anyone you want to be. You're tall so you'll see over them, but you're a nice guy, so you should make friends pretty easy. The playing field is huge and you have to learn to live with rejections. Everyone is different. So, if I were you—"

"He fucks 'em all," Tim interrupted snidely.

"I do enjoy sex, but it's not everyone's cup of tea."

"I think it's my cup of tea if liking sex counts." Danny was so excited he couldn't sit still.

"Don't get him started on all the nasty he's done," Tim warned.

"I have done quite a bit because I'm endlessly curious about men's sexuality."

"That's his way of saying he's a dirty slut." Tim took his empty glass back to the counter to refill it.

"If you like, I could take you to Toad Hall."

"Would you?"

"He'll only know the pretty ones," Tim added.

"I have to run, and I will meet you there at eight." I took my jacket off the back of the chair and left.

Being in the smoke-filled, crowded Toad Hall with Danny

reminded me of my first night in town there. I stood at the wall across from the end of the bar so I could see the men in the back as well as in the front. I was twisted in knots of envy as I watched couple after couple leave the bar. With my vivid imagination, I assumed they were on their way to the apartment of one of them, and I guessed they were going to have sex that I longed to have. They probably didn't know each other, and the result of the first time they had sex I imagined might result in a love that lasted the rest of their lives or they may be lovers until they outgrew each other. For others, I imagined they became friends. I watched them, torn that I didn't know how to ask a man to come home with me, thinking I'd never measure up to the men who walked out with a man. I was defective, and I would end up the sad man nobody wanted to talk to. I decided the men who left the bar with other men had a special quality that made men want to meet them, but I, from little Point Reyes Station, would never have it. I went home alone sad and feeling dejected.

The next day I couldn't get the thought of the two men I saw disappearing up the sidewalk to have sex, who were completely oblivious to me, out of my head. It kept repeating like a broken record. I imagined different scenarios. In one, they have good sex and in the other the sex is so bad, they wished they'd talked to me. I wasn't good enough because nice men asked other nice men to go home with them. I wasn't a nice guy and they could see that.

I somehow rustled up the courage to go back to Toad Hall the next night, and this time I watched Michael behind the bar. He had curly dark hair and the nicest smile I'd ever seen. He had magic, because, with every man asking for a beer, he leaned over the bar and treated them like they were boyhood friends; he did it with complete strangers, and he treated every man the same.

I understood why Tim said I should be careful around Michael because after watching Michael most of the evening in a way I hoped he wouldn't see me, I fell in love with him.

He was the embodiment of everything, I dreamed of in a man. He owned the world that night and he was humble about it. He knew where he was going in life, but he didn't lord it over anyone. I was certain he was the gentle kind of lover I wanted, a man who'd greet me with a smile when I walked in the door and would snuggle next to me in the morning so warmly that I would never want to get out of bed. He was the blood in my veins. I left the bar alone, but thoughts of Michael stayed with me.

The next night he remembered me when I ordered a beer. He even asked, "How ya doin'?" My dream had come true; Michael treated me like a boyhood friend. I was shocked it happened so fast. I frantically watched what other men did after they ordered a beer and Michael treated them as a boyhood friend. If I understood what they did next, I'd have the confidence I needed to ask Michael if he would go home with me. Sadly, after the men were served, they did very different things, but none of them went back to the bar and asked Michael to go home with them. My thinking about Michael and going home with him got so convoluted that nothing made sense. Eventually, certain that he'd never be interested in me, I stopped going to Toad Hall.

A few weeks later, I saw Michael on the street with a good-looking man also dressed in jeans and a flannel shirt. I was certain they were lovers. I would have gone home with either of them and even might consider going home with both of them, but that would never happen. The man with him couldn't be as special as Michael, and I automatically hoped he treated Michael right. But in the back of my mind, I hoped he mistreated Michael so badly that Michael would break up with him. So with some new mysterious powers, I would snatch him up, and Michael and I would live the rest of our lives together. Desire is powerful, and it made me do weird and sometimes stupid things.

Danny wanted to do it on his own, so I'd left him alone. He towered over everyone, so I never lost track of him. There were times when he looked confused. He approached a man and bent over. They talked for a time and, for whatever reason, he smiled and backed off. I saw several men cruise him, but he didn't know what they were doing, so he never saw them. I had a date that night, and just as I was coming up to Danny to say I was leaving, a suddenly bold Danny introduced me to a skinny kid half his size next to him in jeans and a Beatles T-shirt. "Percy just invited me to go home with him. I liked meeting you, Charlie, but I have to go. Maybe another time?"

"That nasty little motherfucker," I muttered. It took me a week of trying and failing to get the dating dance in bars down, but Danny got it that night. I didn't like being shown up by a newcomer.

Over the next couple years, Danny and I ran into each other in various leather bars. Every night we took someone home but because our tastes differed, we never competed. I began to see him as my protégé. We went to a couple old Westerns together.

Danny met Lynn Maes, a veterinarian, at one of Tim's Pride dinners. Lynn claimed he was a quarter inch taller than Danny, but when they stood back to back, Danny insisted they were the same height. They both liked the Nitty Gritty Dirt Band, so they moved in together. A year or so later they bought a home on Eureka Street, which they made their own so naturally that I felt immediately welcome there. Danny loved food, and the meals he prepared in his chef's kitchen were as succulent if less experimental than the meals that Tom and Ted made. They stayed together until Danny died of AIDS complications at the height of the epidemic when it took two pages in the *Bay Area Reporter* to include all the obituaries. By then, I'd lost half my buddies, and I didn't have the emotional strength to attend more funerals, so Danny's memorial service was the last one I attended.

Chapter Nine

The Makings of a Fine Sex Date

1982

I started my career as a player on March 18, Wilfred Owen's birthday. When I first got to San Francisco, I didn't get why the gay men I was meeting didn't know much about sex. I was in the midst of what was reputed to be the nation's epicenter of sexual pleasure, so I expected the men there would know what they're doing with another man when they are having sex. I was on a mission to try everything, so I was also hoping some would know about the kink that I'd heard about. I'd need all the help understanding it I could get. Some men were scientific or spiritual and so seemed to be seeking validation for being gay. That didn't translate into being particularly skilled in bed; they talked a good game.

I didn't think I had super powers, but I was very conscious about what I wanted from sex with a man. I was a close observer, so I paid close attention to every move a man made that made me feel good and some that simply titillated me. I wouldn't call me an expert, but I knew a hellava lot about what made a fine date because I had skin in the game for years. So, if someone was going to put together ideas about what makes the best sex date, why not me?

My subject would be what I did that made for a great sex date, the night or afternoon when two of us got together with the express purpose of pleasuring each other with sex. Not exchanging recipes or celebrity gossip; we got together because we wanted to have sex, not some random blowjob on the side. I think of a sex date as a production with a beginning, a middle, and an end. Over time, routines develop, and on second or third date I would change the routine to freshen it up.

The incredible dates, the ones that blew me away, didn't happen very often. They often caught me off-guard, but within minutes, I knew it was going somewhere tasty and it was going there fast. We started slow to connect, and then we got into the quick hot kinky stuff that we had to get out of our systems. That can be all kinds of positions and tonguing with mouths. That energy built to a crescendo, lingered there, and then we rested. One of us couldn't stop, and we started up a second time. This time it was a deeper connection because we were looser, and at least I wanted to improve on the high I experience d in the first part. That went on for hours, time had no meaning, and it was our bodies that eventually told us it was time to end the play. By then we were sloppy, and we always ended laughing out the joy we'd built up while we were playing. To me, laughing was the sign of the ultimate high.

With every date, from the simplest to the more elaborate, I was the director of the show and it was my responsibility to make sure both of us had a good time. There were dates when I trusted my partner and I gladly gave it up.

Where I played was very important to the outcome of a date. It set the tone. I've been in a lot of dungeons. At one, the guy who lived there had home projects going all the time, so the floors of his apartment were covered with plastic milk crates of parts and loose assemblies, so getting to his dungeon I had to use my stocking feet as Sherpa guides. When I got to the dungeon, I felt I'd accomplished something and that boost balanced off the difficulty in getting there. I've been in grungy spaces like the South of the Slot, but as long as it didn't smell bad, I was fine with putting up with the crud because I had a good chance of getting the sex I wanted.

I had to climb around cars in two steamy-hot garages to get to a play space in Palm Springs, and that first impression put a damper on my attitude. Sex shouldn't be the reward for putting up with complications; your date should be seduced by what he sees from the second he walks in the door. It doesn't have to be a large space, but it does need enough room to move around. A shower's nice and some form of water should be nearby for cleaning up. The best way to design a dungeon is to make one from ideas stolen from the dungeons you've seen. Use your imagination and keep it clean. If a place is dirty, I notice it and I can't enjoy myself.

Place includes everything in it like the lighting and the music. Music enhances the experience and sets the tone. Unless I know the man likes a specific artist, I play whatever's been getting me off emotionally. The first was the Beatles' *Sgt. Pepper's Lonely Hearts Club Band*, then Led Zeppelin's "Stairway to Heaven" and finally Elton John's *Goodbye Yellow Brick Road*. Find music that suits you and your moods. It generally works better when it's not too jarring, music like disco, although guys on speed get off on it, but I avoided guys on speed. Have fun with the music, and try playing with music that meant something to you as a kid. See what those songs bring up. Electronic music is great when you're stoned to the tits. Jean-Michel Jarre's *Equinoxe* album had me drifting through space like a newborn child.

If there isn't a set-aside space for sex, go with the flow. Say your partner wanted the colonial style, over time you've found some lovely colonial bedroom pieces and the bedroom's so perfect, friends want to take pictures of it. Now you have a hot date, and he's on the rough side. What do you do with the colonial bedroom? I think he's going to be more impressed if you leave the room alone and work with the feeling of the room rather than work against it. Covering the comforter on an antique colonial four-poster bed with black plastic to protect it will have them running for the door. Finding a way of working with the style of the room takes extra work, but it's worth it in the end. If he thinks he's been invited into the inner sanctum of a fine home, the effort you put into decorating the room will impress him. He'll feel honored to witness it. Unless he's an asshole, and then you have to ask, "Why did I invite an asshole into a home I put a good chunk of my life and my lover's life into?"

Just hearing insects and rodents in the background puts me on edge. An ambulance siren when he's just about to enter you is a real erection killer, and street noise should be muffled as much as possible. If your apartment in Chicago backs up to the L, there's not much you can do about the L, but you can soundproof the room to a degree with well-placed pillows and strips of dense foam. Again, it takes a lot of work, but you and your date deserve a calm place to have sex, so spend the time and do it right. Over time you'll discover the best way to get the seductive feel you want in your play space and that takes constant tweaking until you get it where you want it. Get it set before the date. There's nothing worse than tweaking stereo equipment with greasy fingers. You don't have to have an expensive set up; just one with clear sound that works so well that once you turn it on, you don't have to think about it. Same with your heater or A/C; they should perform flawlessly. And that means paying attention to them before the date. You don't want to be sweating profusely in a sling and have to slide out and kick the air conditioner with your bare feet hoping that will get it cooling you again.

Lighting should complement the mood, not compete with either you or the décor. Use lights as accents, your play space isn't the dark back room of a bar. I like enough light to see the face of the man I'm having sex with and admire his physique as he takes off his clothes. One playroom was in the home of a lighting engineer, and playing there, I felt I was on a Hollywood set. I looked over my shoulder to see how well he'd done it, and my head cast a perfect shadow on the wall. That made me feel I had to perform for the camera, and I'm not an exhibitionist.

Track lighting works in moderation if you have a dimmer. Lights that sit on the floor can add a dramatic touch if that's what you're after. A buddy on Liberty Street used them in his backyard garden to good effect. Avoid flashing lights that induce seizures in susceptible people.

It was always easy to grab a quickie. It could be on my way home from work or at the end of a long night in the bars. Both of us wanted sex. I did them automatically and they weren't half bad, but that's not a date. A great date requires the same amount of attention as planning a trip to Kauai. If you do it right before the date, the details will take care of themselves and the two of you can relax into a night of pleasure. To be able to be spontaneous during the date requires hours of careful preparation, and don't be ashamed of doing all that work; you and your date will end up having a fine night of sex.

A date should be the result of one's intention, so pay attention to the men you have sex with before, during, and after the date: you have formed a bond. If you have empathy with him, you will connect with him at a deeper level. Treating your date as an object doesn't help anyone, and you can't write anyone off. The more attention I paid to what I wanted to get out of the date before it began, even weeks or months before it began, the better the outcome. I think most of us use sex to satisfy a scar from our youth. In my case, I have abandonment issues from when I was a kid. As long as I'm clear on that, I can use the scar to propel a date rather than letting it derail the date. Sometimes it was nothing more than a flicker to my side. When that scar is hidden and you don't know it's there, it can screw things up because you think you expect one thing from a date but subconsciously you want something else. When our intentions didn't mesh, the date felt unsatisfactory for both of us. Sex should be seamless from beginning to end, so the clearer you are, the smoother the sex. My best sex has always been a mutual exchange between the two of us, not a performance or winning a ribbon.

I knew thundering exhilarations, billows of joy, consuming lust; I flew among planets and rested on slow moving rivers. I was an explosion of happiness. I was a universe of pleasures. Beneath it rested a layer of peat that's composed of years of residual hatred, frustrated dreams, agonizing loneliness, hours of unwanted instruction, years of despair, granules of shattered hopes, and all that shit that collects around them. The level varies from person to person, but if it weren't for the peat, I wouldn't know the highs I experienced when I was having sex and being massaged. They also gave the highs greater depth.

After one date, I asked a man how he was doing. He said, "Why didn't you fuck me?" I'm no mind reader, and he hadn't given me any specific signals or words that he wanted to be fucked, so I gave him a blowjob to remember. Especially when you are in the throes of having sex, don't expect that your date is going to guess what you want. If you're embarrassed to ask and don't ask, that will linger with you the rest of the date

Part of the art of sex is sensing what your partner wants. Men have feelings. It's easy when you're having sex to focus on your crotch and on his crotch, but they connect to deep-seated feelings. Men are not stereotypes. When I first got town and with men showing up all the time, astrology was a handy way to sort them out. But *Linda Goodman's Sun Signs* wasn't always accurate in predicting a person's behavior based on his sign. Each date should be crafted around the man you are playing with and the mood of the times. Each is a delicate work of art, and the more I put into it, the more I get out of it.

Both equipment and supplies are critical. My basic supplies were something to drink, dope, lube, poppers, and a roll of paper towels. I had dark chocolate if we got the munchies. The equipment is where you are going to have sex and everything you are planning to use when you're having sex. If it's an

S/M scene that takes a great deal of preparation, allow time. My friend Stan Hill said setting up his space helped build his excitement. Sometimes after he'd spent hours getting his playroom where he wanted it, the date was a second act.

Beds are the most common places to have sex. Your bed is a stage so it should have a good amount of space to move around it, and what you need while you're on stage has to be there as well. Plastic sheets are easy to clean, but plastic on flesh feels cold and plastic. I used moving pads; they're warm to the touch and I just popped them in the washer if the pads were greasy.

You have an important guest coming, so clean your apartment. I have filthy thoughts when I'm playing, and they can be filthier in a clean room. There were exceptions because libidos can be cruel mistresses.

Remember all the times you wanted something while you were playing, and it wasn't there? Make sure whatever you need when playing is within arm's reach. Unless you think you're being a stud crossing the room with someone's hand in your butt, you don't want to interrupt the symphony of sex with a lot of scrambling around. A great date moves seamlessly, but a great date also requires preparation, otherwise it's just a side show.

If you are going to have butt sex, make sure you have lube close by. For my dates, there was a bowl of lube for him and another for me. If you like slings, make sure yours is securely attached. I fell from one when a screw holding one of the corners popped out of the wall. I fell in his lap, but that shouldn't happen because it stopped the flow. Sex on the floor looks hot in porno when a guy's thrown to the floor and fucked, but floors are hard, and our spines aren't well padded. Climbing around furniture while you're having sex is a lot of monkey fun, but if you know the arm of the chair is loose, avoid that chair and climb around the sofa and the hassock. Hanging Tarzan-like from a chandelier looks impressive, but most chandeliers aren't secured sufficiently to the ceiling to support the weight of a man.

If you are going to have a fire in the hearth, have it properly set with kindling, so all you have to do is strike a match and get back to kissing. If making a fire nude while being watched turns you on, make it a woodsy scene and go for it. Each date is your production, so use your imagination and make it a scene where you feel at your best and maybe exploring some new territory. If you do that, your date will respond in kind and you start feeding off each other. If you're an amateur, admit it. Ask his advice. Seek his wisdom. A date where you're pretending that you know what you're doing when you don't, seldom ends well. A date is a two-way street; my best sex was always a game of give and take.

Role playing lets you tap into parts you've kept hidden. I found they can be quite revealing and often surprising. Respect them for what they are and be clear with your partner on the role you will be playing. If you're confused with your role, he'll be confused. It's also smart to be clear at the beginning because it lets both of you relax into your play and it can also build excitement. Some intentions can be conveyed with gestures, but if there is any question, it's best to say it out loud because then no one's confused while you're playing.

I consider sex a sacred act, so before my date walked through the door, I couldn't be worried about paying the rent. I also had to want to have sex that night with him, a very specific him and day; I wasn't just doing it to kill time. It's critical that you want to have sex when you have sex. That seems logical, but my libido has a mind of its own, and sometimes it wanted to have sex when the rest of me didn't, and that got confusing—and confusion is a real interest killer. On a date with a man I'd wanted to date for years, I thought I could get over what was bugging me about something a friend said, but I couldn't. That made the time we spent awkward for him, and he deserved a hassle-free date where he and our interaction was the focus of attention.

Great sex flows like a mighty river. It's not as easy as it sounds, but the date is going to be far more enjoyable for everyone when both of you are clear on why you are having sex that day. When I was desperate for a quick affection fix, I hurt some men; others were too stoned to care. Your love life shouldn't be a list of regrets; it should be a thick scrapbook of objects, journals, and images that recall wonderful memories.

Your physical state is part of your frame of mind. If you are going to be fucking, make sure you are clean inside as well as outside. Get a good night's sleep. Stay in shape at a gym, do yoga, run a mile every day. When you're playing, moderate your energy so the two of you can play for hours and one of you doesn't wear the other one out. Take breaks. Snack between sets. Sex isn't a race to the finish line.

Drugs were common, and I used them in moderation. Dope was a constant, and I never injected anything, but I've done opium, cocaine, MDMA, and quaaludes. LSD and psilocybin mushrooms were sacred, and I only did them with men who've used them. When I did them with clear intention, they opened my mind and made me a better person.

Thank him. A lot of guys forget to do that. A date should be recognized for playing with you. Even if it didn't turn out exactly the way you wanted it to, thank him. He made the effort to come to your place, and he also did whatever he did to get ready for your date. He deserves to be thanked for it. Some think sex is nasty, and they think thanking a man for his sex is saying you approve of his nastiness. Sex is only as nasty as one thinks it is, and if you think sex is nasty, why do it? If you start a date thinking sex, which I consider is God's gift to gay men, is nasty or unsavory, it will ruin a fine evening.

If you are going to have sex with a man, you should honor the experience from the start through the final shower before he goes home or when he climbs into your bed. I didn't have unlimited days to figure my sex life out, so it was important that I paid attention to what I could do in the time allotted. When I paid attention to why I was having sex with that man, I was uplifted. Being aware of the spiritual nature of sex made it more rewarding for me because I knew we connect with each other spiritually at varying levels while we were having sex. Some say it's rude to rate a date, but when I was aware of what went right and what didn't on a date, I corrected what went wrong so my next date with was seamless.

I hate instructions and I never read that sheet of instructions that comes with appliances. I think sex is good for you, so my goal with sex was getting men comfortable with sex because when both of us were comfortable with it, we had a splendid time together.

I started out a kid from a small town who moved to San Francisco at the right time. So this is not a fool-proof guide but suggestions based on my experience that may give gay men who are new to sex ideas that will make the next sex that you have with your boyfriend or with the stranger you just met a fun experience for both of them.

Chapter Ten

Awakening

An array of Easter-egg red, blue, and yellow tulips surrounded my table at the Patio Café as I waited for William Dean. Will was a large, muscled man who grew up on a ranch in Colorado and had his own graphic design firm that was about two years old. I met Will my first year in town, so I greeted him with a kiss on his lips and a quick hug. "Thanks for coming."

"I'm so glad you're writing a sex manual. I wish there'd been a stack of them when I got here." Wearing jeans and a Grateful Dead T-shirt, William pulled out a bent-wire chair and sat opposite me.

"Some guys are scared of sex."

A cute boy waiter in black jeans, a white shirt, and short white apron asked, "Are you gentlemen ready to order?"

"Do you have that egg and ham grilled cheese?" Will inquired.

"We do indeed. I like your T-shirt. They're my favorite."

"Thank you. I'll have that and a cup of your French roast."

"And what are you going to have today, handsome?"

"The usual," I responded.

"That's one egg ham grilled cheese, two eggs over medium

with bacon, an English muffin, French roast, and Irish breakfast coming up!" He wrote the order on a pad. As he sauntered back to the kitchen I wasn't the only one watching his bubble butt as it slipped side to side.

"Do you have a name for your manual?" Will asked.

"I'd like to keep it simple."

"What do you think of using drawings of legs for the uprights in the letter M on a Manual?"

"It's just my thoughts. The guide is quick and easy."

"That's brilliant; I wish I'd thought of it. I lined up a printer. Tell him how many you want, and he can get it done in a couple days."

"I should be able to get something to him in a week."

The waiter appeared with our orders and put them in front of us. "Will that be all?" he asked, clearly hoping William would say something.

"I think we're fine," I responded. Will said nothing.

"I overheard you, and I'd sure like to get a copy of your sex manual. There should have been one years ago."

"If you give me your card, I'll make sure you get a copy," I said.

"Can I reserve a stack for my friends?" He nervously shifted foot to foot, his excitement shifting to the guide.

"You can have as many as you wish."

"If you don't mind, the first time I went home with a man, nobody told me what to do. There aren't any classes, and I just felt awful. I didn't want to have sex again."

"I'll bet you learned a lot since then." I sensed his enthusiasm.

"Maybe I did." He blushed and grinned at my compliment.

Two weeks later, I was making dinner and the phone rang. "Hello?"

"I'm Kit, you don't know me but I work part-time with Will."

"Is there a problem with the printer?" I could tell he was rattled.

"I'm here in his office, and we're calling everyone in his Rolodex."

"Is Will OK? Was he in an accident?"

"Will died this morning."

"He's dead? How is that possible? He was healthy as a horse when I saw him two weeks ago." I was stunned and had a hard time putting words in front of each other amidst the sobs.

"The doctors don't know what it is."

"How can they not know what a disease is? That's why they spend all that time in fucking med school." I was seething at the incompetence.

"They say they've never seen anything like it. One of them said something about a suppressed immune system. Do you know what an immune system is?"

"Haven't the slightest. It could be a form of VD. He went to the clinic a couple times."

"Sorry to be the bearer of bad news, but I have to keep making calls. Will was such a lovely guy."

"Thanks for letting me know. There isn't a finer man."

That news put me batshit out of my mind. It brought up the rumor of six gay men who shared a summer rental on Fire Island who all died of a mysterious disease within a few months of each other. I had put it off as an East Coast thing. I didn't remember Will saying he'd been on the East Coast, and it was hard to imagine a disease that could leap across three thousand miles.

We were supposed to have the best health system in the world, and they still can't figure out something as simple as the disease's name. Come on! A disease couldn't single out gay men unless we really were genetically different. I decided whatever happened to Will had to be something that the six men ate that killed them.

Shit! My life was built around the men I slept with. They've done nothing so bad that they deserved to die. I thought nature was a perfect world, but killing off innocent men wasn't a perfect world. My buds were healthy as shit, so whatever got Will had to be a fluke.

A month later

I needed answers. Where the fuck were the answers? Scientists discovered things all the time, how could they miss a disease that's killing gay men? It didn't make sense, and I had to trust that the federal government that helped Salk come up with a cure for polio would assemble top-notch scientists and medical professionals to discover the cause of the disease as well as ways of eliminating it. I tried not to worry about getting sick, but I'd had more sex than most men, and there was a lingering feeling that the mysterious disease was somehow linked to sex. But I decided to put off thinking about it until the government announced its plan.

Three months later

I was in full panic mode talking with Sam Skarda, a nurse, at the Stud. "Have you heard anything?" I asked.

"They think it's a virus, and Martin Delany says he's trying to gather the latest information. The stories are all over the place," Sam said.

"Well, where is it?" I asked.

"He's looking everywhere, but he can't find anything."

"You're telling me no one knows what the fuck this thing is?" I didn't understand why highly professional scientists didn't know what was killing gay men.

"The medical establishment won't touch it, and the feds aren't taking it seriously," Sam explained.

"Those bastards! They know it's a virus, but they're letting us die!"

I had to do everything I could to stop this thing from getting to the men who made San Francisco my home. I couldn't let them die, but I felt helpless.

I was curious about my health, so one day in the sauna after my workout, I imagined a miniature Pac-Man in my bloodstream that chomped down on every black dot of the virus it encountered. I ran him through every part of my body, starting with my head. By the time my little guy had run through every vein I could think of, I closed my eyes and looked inside. Looking inside is not as accurate as an X-ray or a CAT scan, but it was the best I could afford. I knew my body pretty well.

I searched methodically and found no disease. I did it twice to make sure there was no disease, and there wasn't. I made a pact with the virus; if I die, you die.

That I had the virus was confirmed when they finally could test for it. I was positive. That I had a good chance of living was confirmed when they could test viral loads, and mine were low.

I decided I wasn't going to sit idly by as men around me died. I was going to find a way of satisfying my need for touch.

Chapter Eleven

"Only you can give me that feeling."
—Anonymous

No one noticed him when Enos entered a room, but I found him sublimely beautiful because I thought his soul was pure. Enos Khoury was my size with black, unkempt hair. He alluded to being into kink, and while I could only guess what kind of kink, the prospect of discovering what kind of kink it was was hard to resist. Over time, as I got to know gay men, I found that geography mattered as did one's upbringing, so I usually started dates by asking them where they grew up and what their family life was like as a kid. I began my date with Enos the same way. In response to my questions, he said he grew up with an older sister in Greenpoint, Brooklyn. His father ran the most successful halal butcher shop in Brooklyn. His mother "ate just enough bacon so Dad let her lead her life as a nightclub singer," he said sarcastically. Because he thought neither of them liked kids, they shipped him off to a military academy in upstate New York, housed in a former World War I base.

"What was that like?" I asked, because after Mom died, I tried to talk Pops into sending me to an all-boys military school so I could see them in the showers.

"My math teacher, Mr. Henderson, stuck his hands in my pants in the teachers' bathroom. When I told Mr. Jovanovich, the stick-in-the-mud headmaster, that Mr. Henderson raped me, he accused me of making it up because he said Mr. Henderson was their most popular teacher. I wondered if I should have used another word than rape," Enos explained.

"Oh, my God! How horrible." This was way beyond anything I'd experienced.

"I still smell his breath when I'm in a men's room. The good part is that being in military school, I developed my interest in making things. When I wasn't in my room with the finished product, I was in the maintenance facility picking through drawers of parts."

"You did that and they never said anything?" I couldn't believe anyone could get away with that.

"My father promised the headmaster he'd make a generous donation if I graduated. How's paying off to get me graduated for fatherly love?"

"That's an awful thing for a father to do. What did you make?"

"The first thing I made was a pocket radio, and then I made a wind-powered electric cell that produced enough power to charge the radio so I could listen to the radio. Late at night, I could get those scratchy AM stations. I stopped wearing pink because a man on one of them said pink was the color homosexuals used to identify each other in communist countries. My most ambitious was a Jeep."

"A fucking Jeep!? You believed that pink commie malarkey?" I was embarrassed that I never made anything.

"I did at the time. Now it's downright stupid. I sold the Jeep."

"You wanna get naked?'

"Don't you want to know about what made me so much money?" He wetted his lips with vodka tonic.

"Money's nice, but I don't think it's a big deal."

"You're missing out; fortunes are being made overnight.

You just have to apply yourself. You could do it, and I know you'd like it. Mine wasn't as nearly as big as Jobs' or Gates' but it made me a millionaire several times over."

"I give up. What was it?" I was beginning to feel the date was a mistake and it was time to come up with an exit strategy.

"I was awarded a patent for a circuit design that vastly improves Windows connectivity."

"You're very talented." I felt like an amateur because I didn't know what that meant, but I didn't want him thinking I was a dumbass.

I'd never seen such a quick change in a man, but once the boasting was out of his system, Enos turned into a man who knew what he was doing with a man in bed, and he wasn't shy about taking the lead. I trusted him, so when he began stroking me, he was chamois cloth and I soaked up his touch. Once we were in bed, his genius was not limited to technology because he showed me a way of lying on our sides that made our lovemaking completely different.

Over the next few months, he continued to show his softer side to me, and I tried several times to figure out why I was so attracted to him. Enos had limited experience in the San Francisco playing field that can be kinda rough, and as someone who'd been around the block, I felt I was responsible for showing him what to expect and how to cope. It was the first time I ever felt responsible for someone, and it felt good to think of him as the younger brother I never had. I was also intrigued with his mind that I was sure was larger than mine. I marveled that his mind saw the world completely differently than I did because I thought most minds basically thought along the same lines. When I mentioned that Pops kept tide charts, he said, "Did you know that Sir William Thomson devised the method of reduction of tides by harmonic analysis in 1867?"

How did Enos know that?

I expected I'd be bored when he showed me a circuit board, but the way he described what each minute part of it did, it kept me fascinated. That so much data could be crammed into tiny filaments of quartz seemed impossible. I was never going to be a scientist, but I thought I should know something about science because technology was increasingly everywhere. I thought his kink would be leather, and as I often was with him, I was wrong.

He arrived on time for our fourth date as he did the first time. Promptness was important, he told me. This time he brought a small duffel bag that he put on the hall floor when he took off his jacket. We sat at the kitchen table and drank Manhattans that he made with a mix he brought. I'd never had one, and they were too sweet for me, but they were potent and I got tipsy. We smoked a joint, and when we started kissing he was voracious. We left a trail of discarded clothing from the kitchen to the bedroom. With the music I set up playing in the bedroom, he told me to keep my underwear on while he got something. I thought that was kind of a strange thing to do at the start of a date. He left and came back with the duffel bag. He opened it on the bed and, like popcorn in theaters, pair after pair of mostly white underwear spilled out of it. Some were torn, some piss-stained, others were narrow European cuts, and some elaborate G-strings. He asked me if I would model a pair and handed me a pair of torn BVDs. I took mine off and when I was in that pair, my pubes stuck out. He had me turn around, and I saw he was aroused by what he saw. He fondled my dick beneath the cotton as if it were a sacred object before he let me take them off. I'd never known anyone so obsessed; I felt I was watching a movie.

We spent the rest of the evening going through his collection of underwear, with both of us donning various pairs. Sometimes we modeled them for each other. Once the ones that I was wearing excited him, and after nuzzling them, he ripped them to shreds and stuffed them in his mouth. Like fog that slowly creeps up on you, his fascination with underwear and erections enveloped me. I ended up doing some crazy stupid stuff with him in underwear of different conditions, and I came to understand the meaning of fetish.

No one had ever treated me to anything. Not to dinner, not even a movie, but Enos treated me to a weekend at a weathered, shingled cottage nestled in a densely-wooded hillside at Big Sur. The dense growth and the quaint cottage made me feel like I was an elf in an elf world while I was there. We were supposed to soak in separate tubs overlooking the Pacific, but I got in his to snuggle. As we snuggled in the hot water from natural hot springs in the hills behind us, waves pummeled the dramatic promontory below us in fierce lashes. I thought I knew the Pacific pretty damn well, but as it crashed on the rocks below us, I had new respect for the sea's power. Teams of black swifts darted in kamikaze formations perilously close to each other without ever touching. After catching dinner on the fly with amazing accuracy, they fluttered to their mud nests in the cliff face outside the window and fed their young. A humpback whale breached sending a fountain of spray, and I remembered wanting to migrate with them on those warm spring days when I was a kid with no cares and who dreamed of running away from home. I ate a simple, beautifully prepared poached salmon filet under an ornate paper lantern atop another promontory at Nepenthe restaurant, where elegantly attired hippies with silver jewelry served as our wait staff. They weren't serving me just food, they took me on a journey that was just as seductive as the food, which was always the perfect temperature. That night we did LSD, and as I lay on his belly under the arching Monterey pines with my nostrils saturated with Pacific salt, I tripped in a far-off kaleidoscope of color and magical creatures. Our sex was ethereal, and just when I thought I couldn't take more, Enos said, "I love you."

I melted; I was puddle, mud, formless. No one had ever said they loved me, and I didn't believe that I was worth loving. I didn't think I could love him back because love for me had been movies and something that only unattainable people did. Then I wondered, was that wooziness I'd been feeling when I was around him love? When his love stared me in the face, I knew I loved him, but because my love felt fragile, I didn't tell him, fearing that it would go away if I did.

I suddenly needed Enos, and I couldn't be more than five feet away from him. Feelings of losing control and being unable to think for myself were ugly feelings that I resisted, but they made me feel unworthy and held me like a vise. Whenever they washed up, I tried to replace them with the way his robin-egg-blue eyes looked into me and the warmth welled up in me, but they kept coming back.

Being in love was a crazy feeling I couldn't control and didn't want to control. Enos was a magician. I'd never felt so unmoored. Whenever we were together, I wanted to live snuggled next to him the rest of my life.

Chapter Twelve

"Love is not a victory march."
—Leonard Cohen, singer-songwriter

Enos and I celebrated our fourth anniversary with friends around a table at Zuni Café. My friends had a knack of finding just the right present, something they knew I would like, not necessarily something expensive, but they were unique, and I would always remember where it came from.

I thought I was happy, but happiness was hard to define and meant different things to different people, so I was never sure I was happy. Enos was quite content being solitary; his issues were his, and disturbing him made him nervous. His nervousness put me on edge and it sometimes killed our playing. Our biggest fight was over marriage. Enos wanted us to have the right to marry, and I understood there were legal benefits and customs to be honored. My love for Enos was pure, but it was also tenuous in my eyes, and I didn't want to lose it. At the same time, I knew if I was confined by a certificate or a ring I'd bolt and get the hell out of Dodge.

Enos never understood me when I said I was emotionally monogamous. When I was playing, I was fully engaged with my date, but my steady love of Enos ran strong below that. I felt I would be a hollow shell without Enos. I wished that he could have understood that my emotional life pivoted around him and his physical and psychological needs. I wished he understood that waking with him next to me gave me strength to weather whatever shit got thrown at me.

When we made love, I was joined to another soul, the most beautiful feeling in the world. There was none of that with the men I played with. Nothing compared to our one-on-one lovemaking, because with Enos, there was a blending of hearts. Because of him, I risked a steady income and quit the mayor's office that I'd joined, foolishly thinking I could do something for the community but was stymied at every attempt by a politician's ego. I started consulting with non-profits. It was rough at first, but it came together.

The last four years we were together, I matured more than I had in any similar period. If one looked around the condo I co-owned with him near the top of Nob Hill, at the art on the walls, the magazines on the coffee table, and the porno mags in the basket in the bathroom, one would never have accused us of being boring, middle-class acquisitive because all of it was clearly homocentric. A man said we were a model gay couple, and I accepted that with due modesty because it wasn't true; we were just as fucked up as most couples because from the way I grew up, I thought being fucked up was basic human nature.

The last year we were together, I was invited to a play party. Because Enos didn't like them, I didn't ask him to join me.

The party was held on the Sonoma ranch of Curtis Gale, who invented a switch that made communication a thousand times faster between two miniature somethings in a computer I never understood, but it made him a ton of money overnight. I'd heard his ranch was a one of a kind, so I had to see it. Curtis was in his mid-fifties with the body he made at the gym when he was twenty, but I noticed immediately that he was uneasy with his sexuality. That explained why he must have spent a fortune outfitting the barn that had every possible high-end sexual device and play thing, like a Rolls-Royce playroom that a gay man would sell his left nut for. There was enough space to separate all of the specialties into accessible arrangements. So, unlike some of the playrooms I'd been in, as I surveyed it I knew I wouldn't be knocking over a can of Crisco or hitting my head on a low ceiling.

He did it wrong. Most dungeons were painted black, but he used light bright colors, so if I played in it, I'd feel like a carnival clown, not the actor in an out-of-focus porno movie I thought I was when I played in dark dungeons. A corner of the barn had a St. Andrew's cross, a wall of ropes to tie men against, and a fuck bench, all covered in black leather. It looked like none of it had ever been touched. What looked like a gun closet had racks of leather outfits and drawers of dildos that ranged from pencil thin to calf-birthing huge. He said he had a crew steam clean everything before the party, but I wasn't going to put on a jock strap when I didn't know its history. The slings were individually hung from 2" × 4" wood frames. Each had a stainless-steel stool and a red molded-plastic table next to it with a ceramic container of lube, a bottle of expensive poppers, and a fresh roll of paper towels. They were so neat and clean that they were fucking creepy. I thought sex should be a mystery and everything about it should be mysterious. A small corner with a low ceiling had crimson walls and padded wood lounges like a retro Roman bath. I spent much of the afternoon there tired of pretending to have fun at his charade asking myself why am I was obsessed with how other men deal with sex? I'd had so much phenomenal sex, I should have left it at that.

I shared a room with a burly man from Connecticut in the Bunkhouse decorated in what I called late Roy Rogers. The room was typical motel size with cowboy-themed bedspreads and cowboy-boot lamps. The closet was twice the size of mine at home, a not so subtle reminder that Curtis desperately wanted to impress friends.

After stowing my things, I wanted to be helpful and asked

Curtis if I could put out the deck chairs around the pool. While his normal voice had some music, his response to my offer was monotone, "My family went to Tampa every February so my parents could play bridge. They deposited me at the dreary compound's pool and its withered shells of residents that looked like they'd been poured into those nasty plastic lounge chairs. If men need to sit, they can do it in their room."

"That's gonna be kinda hard."

"I wanted the white sand beach on Mykonos, but only the boys were for sale."

"You tried to buy the whole fucking beach? You pulled that from your ass; I don't believe you. Were the boys your consolation prize?"

"Me with a sixteen-year-old? I would never be caught dead." He confirmed that men's pettiness knows no boundaries.

Two of my buddies were at the party, Leslie from Tennessee and Marcel from France. We liked each other and we played well together. Some words like "Aw fuck!" are universally understood, so I spent a rousing afternoon with them. We began slowly, reminding each other why we liked playing together. We showed each other our tricks, and best of all, we reminded each other how much we loved each other. When the three of us sat down to dinner in a hall with a vaulted redwood ceiling, I was still vibrating. That made the trip worthwhile.

Looking around the expensively appointed hall as dessert was served, I knew I'd go bonkers if I had what Curtis had and I lived there alone. I saw no evidence of anyone permanent beyond the kitchen staff and two groundskeepers. I wondered what Curtis felt as he surveyed his splendid property. Did he appreciate nature's incredible bounty or was he disappointed that the spectacular views didn't tuck him in at night? I knew I'd shrivel up and die if I lived there alone as he did.

Sharing warmth with friends was better than I expected of the weekend, so the next morning when everyone was playing in the barn, I slipped out after leaving Curtis a thank you under a cowboy-boot lamp and drove back to San Francisco.

When I got home, Enos was at work. I spent the afternoon wandering around flower beds on trails layered with redwood bark in Golden Gate Park. In the Polo Field, a red-tail-hawk in the highest branches of an oak waited for errant cotton-tail to make a mistake. Koi fought for position when they were being fed in the koi pond at the Japanese tea house. Their differences reminded me of how lucky I was to live in a city of rich diversity.

Chapter Thirteen

Nothing Good Lasts Forever

1983

When Enos came home, he lit into me with the fury an injured tiger. It wasn't the first time; our struggles over my promiscuity had been ongoing. Having sex with friends and the occasional stranger was as much a part of me as being five foot eleven. The first half of my life I'd stifled that urge, locked it deep inside, but once the genie was out of the bottle there was no putting it back. I tried going without thinking of sex, briefly, before I came out, and the results were disastrous; I was cranky and I hated myself for tearing up my only naked boy magazine in disgust. I also I gained weight, a lot of weight. In three months, I put on ten pounds of belly fat. We don't get do-over cards in this lifetime, and there was no way in hell that I would ever be monogamous with anyone, so our squabbles over my promiscuity became the leitmotif of our relationship.

One of the greatest things about coming out was that I could be honest, and I thought I'd done a pretty good job of coming out without hurting anyone except Pops. It was hard for Enos when I told the truth, as it would be for any man, and

I gave him credit for getting to a place where our squabbles became the way we communicated; I didn't like it, but it worked.

Lake Tahoe

Enos straddled me on the deck like the Colossus of Rhodes, if the Colossus had a cute butt. He swiveled to his second home, a rose-colored Indian marble-faced mansion behind him. "I'm going to miss her," he said with nostalgia.

I didn't believe him and pushed him into the lake so clear I could see the bottom. He was pissed when he got out, making a pool of lake water at his feet.

"What the fuck? Can't you take a joke?" I asked.

He nodded at the purple blotch on his leg. "That's KS."

"You said they were blood blisters." I was temporarily blinded by strands of long auburn hair.

"They're KS."

Fuck! I was scared as shit Enos was dying, so I pushed the strands aside and babbled as fast as I could, "You're not going to die! You want to go back to the gym? You know what? We should go to Hawaii and stay at that resort on Kauai. You'd have nothing to do but soak up sun, and when you're well enough, you can swim with the dolphins. Then when you're even better, we'll go to the surfer beach. Remember the furry blond there with the big board?"

"That's not funny. Doc Brach says I have two months at best. Please spare me a memorial service and, God forbid, a pointless funeral!"

I straightened up on my elbows. "You're not going to die. But if you did, I'll want to remember you. Your client list is pretty long, and they will want to remember you. You owe those of us who love you the chance to honor your memory." Embarrassed that I'd said something shallow, I flicked a tick burrowing into my thigh belly first into the lake.

"Shut up! Shut up! Can you do it my way for once?" His eyes glared dark.

"There will be absolutely no service!" I pulled him to me and kissed him sweetly.

He broke, saying, "I turned over the business to Steve, but I must keep others from getting sick, so I'm gonna find out what I can do for Shanti when I get back." His jaw held steady as he headed to the house.

"And you will be their bestest ever volunteer," I declared as I followed him into darkness.

Six weeks later

Back in the city, I was home after trying to settle my differences with the health department over VD testing, my first effort to stem the tide of the epidemic. The corroded bureaucratic minds at the Health Department thought that the city's free VD clinic on Fourth Street was the only place the VD tests could be done. The queer Metropolitan Church was doing the tests, and they stationed a nurse at a folding table in the sanctuary. He pricked fingertips to get droplets of blood that he put in a vial. That's all he did. The properly wrapped vials were then sent to a specialty lab at Stanford that was super-hygienic and used the most current technology to read the blood to see if there is any evidence of gonorrhea or syphilis. I argued what was so wrong with what they were doing, especially when safe sex was the word of the day, but they didn't buy it.

I stomped my feet to clear my head and laid my jacket over the back of the hall chair. "Bohemian Rhapsody" wafted from the bedroom, and I knew it was that goddamn clock radio that a disgruntled engineer in Hiroshima had purposely designed it so that I, Charlie McKey, would never figure it out.

I dropped my keys in the dish on the hall table and noticed an envelope with my name in Enos' script leaning against it. He never wrote letters, so I assumed the letter was his loving way of saying that he needed time alone. Much as I hated waking without him, if those were his wishes, I had to honor them because he was dealing with KS. Making a stink would make it worse, and I should be keeping him alive. I ran my hand through my hair as I checked myself in the hall mirror. I worked up a smile and picked the envelope up with my thumb and first finger. It was sealed, so I got the letter opener on my desk, sat in the chair with a tear in the arm, and slid the sharp edge of the opener through the top of the envelope. I spread it open to a folded sheet of paper and my heart skipped a beat at the thought that he'd taken a full page to explain why he needs time alone. I unfolded the letter and snapped it open and my hands were shaking. Once they stopped shaking I began reading.

Dearest Charlie,

You are the kindest man, and I never thought I'd ever know someone like you, and I know it is highly irrational but I fell in love with you.

When I started working with my Shanti buddy Rocky Teeter, I thought someone as young and strong as him was going to pull through. I used him as a guinea pig with the vegetarian diet the Shanti doctor recommended because most vegetarian food tastes like cardboard. I bought spices like fenugreek and ginger, and even though Rocky said he hated vegetables and that he lived on what he bought at the corner store, he liked the roasted chicken I made. All was going well, he was eating and sleeping soundly, and then on that hot day we had in September when the temperature was 91, when I opened the door to his apartment I had to cover my nose because I thought he'd painted the room with shit. He was sitting in a pool of diarrhea dripping off the bed sobbing. His bed clothes were soaked and I got it on my shoes, so I didn't want to hold him. He was holding his gut from the pain, and because he's afraid of getting addicted, he refused serious pain killers, so it took me the afternoon feeding him aspirin to get his bedroom halfway decent so he could sleep.

He refused to be taken to General or even have me call a doctor. How does a twenty-five-year-old turn into a grumpy grandpa? When the pain subsided, I tried to talk him into us going for a walk but he refused. A week later he got so wasted he was skin and bones, so every time he needed to go, I had to carry him to the john and hold him when he pissed or took a shit. I couldn't get the smell out, and I tried everything, but I still smelled like the bottom of an outhouse. I took a long shower to get rid of the smell of his undigested food the night you were in Palm Springs. You say you want a home there in the winter but that's an excuse to have sex with your buddies. You could have told me, and I would have tried to understand because I loved you.

On my last visit his blankets were strewn on the floor so after I took his temperature of 101, I folded them. When I went to get an aspirin in the bathroom I saw a box of needles and little ratty bags of white powder in the cabinet. When I see a man ruin a beautiful life with speed, it crushes everything I believe in.

This is taking me a long time to write because it's hard to write this, and I still haven't told you everything. A couple weeks ago, my stomach was cramping so bad I couldn't walk, and I didn't want end up like Rocky, so I stopped the AZT. The cramps got better, and the wheat grass shakes I've been drinking made me want to live and I had a couple of good days.

We had such a good night last night I expected my blood work would show a big jump. I got them this morning, and I have no T-cells.

I have thought about this for a long time because I knew this day would come, and it hurts to say this to the man I love, but it makes no sense for me to go on like this, and you don't need me around when I'm that sick. I swallowed the pills I got from the Hemlock Society ten minutes ago, and I am going to lie down.

You're the best, and I love you bunches,
Enos

Enos was dead! Time stopped! The letter dropped to the floor.

*

Enos was within me, but he wasn't in the corpse on the bed. I should have stopped playing around long ago. I didn't understand why the universe that had provided for years would turn on us. What had we done to deserve it? Hunched over my desk, my tear-soaked mind was blank because Enos was in the Great Bathhouse in the Sky, where gay men go when they die but I was alive. I reverted to not thinking, just observing the dark alleys and Greyhound terminal urinals of memory. I didn't have to eat food or wear clean underwear because nothing mattered; I was just a scared little kid facing the scariest thing I'd ever faced.

Enos' death peeled off a layer, so I had less protection going forward. Without Enos, I was the bricks of a foundation that were beginning to crumble but still strong enough to support the building. I was a visionary, but no one would want to live with a man who saw the future but lived in the past. I could have joined the Alice B. Toklas Democratic Club but my gut didn't have a soft spot for it.

I would grieve Enos until the day I died, but I couldn't wallow in it; Enos wouldn't have wanted that. I asked Tim to help me scatter his ashes on the beach at San Gregorio, and he agreed, sobbing, "He was so young."

On the drive down the coast, I was going backwards because one of my happiest days with Enos was the day he and I made the coolest shelter on the beach at San Gregorio from the driftwood strewn by winter storms along the beach. The beach seemed to stretch forever and walking along the shoreline jumping back from waves, I was at one with living things along the shore, like the tiny white crabs that skittered when I neared them, the clams I knew by their holes in the sand, and the sand dollars with their round shells. Snowy plovers and gulls pecking at tiny bugs flew off as I got closer. I lolled in the heat in the shelter while outside, Enos sculpted an anatomically correct life-size green turtle from wet sand.

Feeling special in the shelter, I ate a scrumptious lunch of a thin sliced ham and Gruyère sandwich and a carrot and raisin salad that Enos made. We ended our perfect day making love in his thin flannel sleeping bag in the shelter to the sounds of the waves.

Crouching next to a tidal pool of tiny crustaceans as the sun began to set, I removed the plastic bag of ashes from the blue box. Tim started putting stubby little candles around the the pool, but my gut roiled with emotion, so I opened the bag, took a handful of ashes whispering, "Let's get this fucker over with." I scattered handfuls of ashes three times, and what was left of Enos was caught by a breeze and bounced towards the heavens.

Years later, when I had the Internet, I found the lyrics to "Bohemian Rhapsody" and I broke down hearing *Gotta leave you all behind and face the truth*. Because he couldn't say it in person, the song was Enos' way of saying his final good-bye.

Chapter Fourteen

We All Make Mistakes

1987

The epidemic took a terrible toll on men's minds, and most of the men I played with were dead. Jake, a buddy I played with every month, moved to Oregon with a lover. Oliver and James, two younger buddies I'd played with regularly, had differences. They were sharp with each other. I couldn't play with them and their anger, but it made me sad to see lovely men at odds with each other. I shifted my anger at AIDS up several notches, and my interest in sex decreased.

I never expected it wouldn't be there.

I was starved to be touched when I met long-haired Franc Shepefev, who was playing in a quartet at an afternoon concert in the Conservatory of Flowers, making beautiful music. I didn't know any musicians, so I wasn't sure what I should say to him, but after they stopped, I said, "That's a beautiful instrument, but I can't figure out what it is."

"It's my grandfather's viola." He turned toward the sun to show me its workmanship.

"Sorta like a violin."

"But sweeter." He held it in his arm like a child.

I introduced myself. He told me his name and said he'd just gotten into town.

I spent a couple hours with him over espresso and hand-made donuts at a shop in the Sunset run by lesbians. He had the face of a cherub, but his clothes were grubby. He told me he studied with a master in Vienna, and that he had played on the street in New York while he lived with several other musicians in the East Village. He was reluctant to talk about his parents. His gorgeous music and the way he looked at me made me want to know him better, and I invited him home. He put his viola in a battered case and he came home with me.

That night in bed, he unleashed a whirlwind of passion, and he was all over me like it was 1972. He had more energy than some of the men I'd played with, but our play didn't have the depth that making love to Enos had.

There was a calm insistency with Enos. He was very present, and he could also be a sweet little boy. Enos saw sex as something to be mastered, like music theory, and I was his instrument. Most of the time he was serious and miles ahead of where I was thinking. But when he was having sex, he became innocent and curious. That playfulness was in sharp contrast to his laser focus on his inventions that consumed him. There was never a dull moment with Enos, who jumped from idea to inspiration to turning an idea into reality. They all happened in flashes. I thought he loved me, and I saw his softer side. Making love to Enos was being inside a fully inflated dirigible in a thunder storm.

Franc wanted to get everything he could out of me, going as deep as he could to reveal secrets I'd tucked securely away years ago. His goal seemed to be getting as far inside me as he could. I wondered if I offered him strength, or did he think of me as a curiosity? Was he expecting to find an answer to his quest in me? Or, did he want me to fully expose myself? Was he daring me to do it? And if I had done that, if I had opened myself completely to him, would he use that to absorb the energy I was giving off, or did he want to have control over me? Sad experience had taught me that the men who felt that way were covering for feelings of inadequacy.

Once I was in bed with Franc, I was too desperate for touch to start slow, so our energies took off. We crazed around, built it to an apex, and because I wasn't climaxing, we lingered there not knowing what he was thinking or feeling before bringing it down in the room infused with the soft smell of dope, the chemical smell of poppers with a note of Crisco. His craziness was so exceptional I wanted to repeat the craziness. But this time was more intense, so we crazed around again, doing things I had never done until one of us outlasted the other and we collapsed. I thought I'd run the gamut of sexual positions, and my vocabulary of utterances during sex was extensive, but Franc ripped up the vocabulary rule book. By the time we'd finished playing, the bed was a mess.

If Franc could, I'm sure he would have tried to slide inside my skull, and I was curious about him wanting to do that. I was not concerned about what he'd find; what he found might have some value. My concern was the nature of the hole he was trying to fill or the wound he was trying to salve.

One of the reasons I went home with so many men, besides being touched by them, was that I wanted to understand the workings of gay men's minds. Part of it was to reassure me I wasn't mentally ill and part of it was simple curiosity. I kept being surprised by how different and beautiful we were. I didn't know if I could have done it with my straight friends, but gay men wanted to talk about what they were feeling and why they reacted to a situation. They weren't hemmed in by tradition and feelings, and they divulged personal issues that I once thought were only divulged to psychiatrists. I'd met over a thousand men, and each of them had their own mental constructs and their own array of feelings.

Recognizing this was helpful when I played, because I had a better idea of how something I did or said would be accepted, and by avoiding those that I thought were problematic, our play stayed focused on our play. Playing was the most intimate way I could connect with another man, and I wasn't nice to men who abused that.

Franc's mind, from what I gathered, worked at a different level than any of the men I'd played with including Enos. Instead of sensing his uniqueness as a warning and cutting off the relationship, I thought that since I hadn't ever fully understood Enos, I foolishly thought I'd do a better job of understanding Franc. I invited him to move in with me.

Before I did that, I should have asked if he'd had any lovers and found out something about his past relationships. So when he walked through the door with a suitcase, I would know more about him and what he'd packed in that suitcase. I never did that, but I gave him the key to my apartment and access to my soul. That was stupid.

A week or so after he moved in, I took him out to dinner. As we were being seated, I saw a friend and I kissed and hugged him as I did with all of my friends. Before I sat, Franc was furious, demanding to know, "What's so great about him?"

I tried to explain that I always greet my friends by kissing and hugging them, but he was indignant, acting as if I'd promised him that I would live the rest of my life with him. "That's no way to act. What kind of a man are you?"

Questioning my masculinity always put me on the defensive and I don't think straight. I made the second mistake. I thought if I was nice to him, he'd drop his anger that seemed directed at everything he had contact with. After his next snit, I went out of my way to avoid greeting friends and made sure he was the center of my attention. As long as I did that, I was rewarded that night with a round of furious sex that, for a while, I was ready to accept because I was being touched.

One night as I lay exhausted after playing, he talked about his dream of playing with the San Francisco Symphony.

Giorgio Antonino, a sex mate I'd met at the baths years ago, worked for the Symphony, so I took him and Franc out to lunch at Hayes Street Grill. Throughout the meal, they were engrossed in a conversation about music, little of which I understood, but they were actively engaged. Giorgio must have been impressed with Franc because he arranged to have him audition with the Symphony's first violin, a woman named Evelyn.

When Franc came back from the audition, he didn't thank me. Acting like a little kid with his first bike, he proudly boasted, "She was impressed. I saw it in her eyes. I knew this day would come."

"Congratulations."

That night, he was even more passionate in bed. While I showered, I patted myself on the back for plucking a man who'd lived on the street and depositing him on the route to musician stardom.

The response to his audition came in the form of a letter a couple weeks after the audition that I mistakenly opened because all the mail had been always mine. The letter from the symphony's personnel director mentioned Franc's native talent and thanked him for taking time to audition. She went on to say that if he was serious about becoming a member of the symphony he would need to spend at least two years in one of several training programs. She added an attachment that listed the programs and ways to contact them.

Later, Franc came home fussing over being slighted by a clerk in a store. Sitting down to dinner, he said, "They hire morons, and I'm never going there again. Did I get a call? Why are they taking so long to get back to me? That was my best performance of that piece, and she loved my mastery."

"You shouldn't pin your hopes on one audition. I don't know the business, but don't a lot of musicians try several times before they got noticed?" The letter was under my leg.

"I just told you that was the best performance of my life." He eyed me suspiciously, as if whatever happened was going to be my fault.

"I'm sure it was your best and I'd guess they probably see other fine players, too." I was afraid if I told him the truth, he'd go mental on me.

"You don't think I'm good enough!" He glared at me and slammed his plate on the floor, breaking it into shards. He glared at me, and when I didn't say anything, he stormed out of the room like a runaway train and locked himself in my bedroom, where we'd be sleeping.

I finally had to get down on my hands and knees and plead through the key hole to get him to open the door. But after hours of pleading, I gave up, pissed at my stupidity for thinking he would change.

The next morning, he came out in a pair of my jeans and my favorite shirt. He took his jacket from the hall closet and his viola and left, I assumed to practice, as he had been doing in a practice room at the Academy of Music. I knew he was angry, but I tried to put it out of my mind. That afternoon I went to the market for groceries. When I went to pay the cashier, I found I had no wallet. Shit! The thief stole my wallet. Could he have taken more? Back at the apartment, I discovered that he'd also stolen the gold pocket watch that Enos gave me.

I'd been duped by Franc's music and his skills in bed, and I didn't want to expose my mistake to anyone because I had a reputation as a player that had his shit together. The sad advantage I had from the epidemic was there were fewer people who knew me. For months, whenever I saw the ads for the Symphony on TV, I cringed. It took me over a year to stop blaming myself for not cutting it off sooner. After that, I was cynical and just the thought of loving someone scared me.

Chapter Fifteen

Enough!

2003

Fog licked roofs and I was chilled by the fall air but warmed by the effort it took climbing the hill. I hadn't seen Tim years.

In my fifties, I took on the role as older mentor. I felt I should be the helper my talented teachers had been for me, but the men I was having sex with hadn't come to San Francisco as I had after a life of total repression. They had role models in Boy George and Dave Kopay while I'd had none. AIDS colored everything, so I thought they lacked soul. When I got to be in my sixties, sex stopped being fun and it was no longer the vital part of my life that it had been. At sixty-eight, I finally hung up my spurs and stopped having sex.

Since I last saw Tim, I'd had a series of consulting jobs, mostly with companies that were diversifying their company for the first time. The one that opened my eyes was a carpet company that had been in the family for close to ninety years. The great-grandson Joseph Donatello III was running the company. I met him suited up nicely with a rooster tie behind a desk in an office that looked straight out of a '30s movie with glass panels above wood ones. I expected him to be fixed in his way since he had only begrudgingly agreed when his board that said the company had to be more representative of the community. I'd seen it before. He asked me if I wanted coffee or tea. I asked for tea, and he summoned his secretary, a bright young Asian woman, who politely asked if I wanted milk and sugar.

He offered me a seat in a captain's chair that had seen decades of butts. I sat and shortly after telling her what I wanted, she returned with a steaming cup with the tag and string over the rim that she put on a little side table.

"Would you like anything else?" she asked.

"I'm fine, thanks."

"We gotta problem here, and I'm hiring you to give me answers to them," Mr. Donatello bellowed.

"What can I do for you?" I asked, surprised, because I came equipped with a mental list of thoughts about changing the current make-up of his staff as I did with every job.

"I want to know what people your age think of San Francisco. I grew up in Forest Hills and that was a long time ago."

"Would you like me to review some suggestions for diversifying your staff?" I asked as I'd asked others several times.

"You don't have to tell me that. I know my staff. Let me repeat what I said, I want to know what people your age think of the city."

"Well, I'm sure what I think is going to be different from what Latino people think."

"It damn well better be. My neighbors growing up were the Gilberts, the Snows, the Chinns, and the Delgatos. If we could have found a black couple, we would have found a place for them. That mixture of people and cultures is what I have always loved about the city. With all these techies coming in, I want to know if that has changed, what people think about the city."

"Excuse me, but aren't you really interested in what they think of your product?" I used words straight out of the how-to book.

"Please know that we've been asking that question for four generations. It started with my great-grandfather, Gustavo Donatello. He'd been in the country long enough to be settled and he wanted to know what people in the city thought about it. He got a group of men like himself together. They were all immigrants, some new to the country and all were new to the city. One was Irish, two were German, there was an older man from Mexico who'd lived here most of his life, and there were a Russian and two Chinese gentlemen. He built his business around what they said about what they thought about the city. As you can see, that was a pretty smart thing to do. My grandfather continued the tradition, and my father hired a survey team and what they gave him was dogshit, so he assembled a group of what he considered leaders and then set up meetings with each of them, and he scandalized some by including women. That's a great tradition, and I'm honored to be part of it."

"You're paying me to tell you I think San Francisco's the best possible place for a gay man like me."

"That's what I wanted to hear, and I want you to get ten people in your community to answer that same question. Then you collect them, summarize what you've found, and put that in something I can read. It doesn't have to look expensive."

"I'll do my best, and thank you for choosing me."

Tim had moved from his third-floor apartment to the first floor. I didn't know what to expect. He met me at the door in a thick, indigo terrycloth bathrobe and he used a cane. "Come in. Come in. I moved down here so I'm only on one level. It's easier to get around." He slouched on the sectional. "I also did it to get away from the noise. If you ever own property, make sure you only rent to people who are forty or older. Forty is the last chance to shit or get off the pot, and that's when they decide to be responsible adults. They take care of where they live. Are you still drinking sparkling water?"

"I'd like juice if you have it."

"There's a can in the fridge."

I took one out of the fridge, opened it, and sat on the same chair I'd sat in my first time opposite him, now prone on the sectional that he'd reupholstered. "I can't remember the last time I saw you, but I hear you've been busy. You were going to do everything. How far did you get?" he asked, lifting his head.

"You're probably not any more interested in the jobs I had than I am."

"Tell me about the men in your life."

"All of them?" I asked jokingly.

"The important ones."

"You know about Thomas. Ted and Tom, identical twins who lived in Sonoma, were my first friends. I was serially monogamous for a while."

He grimaced, looking at the ceiling his fist clenched. "Do you hear that? It's the damn kids in two-oh-five."

"Are they noisy all day? I had a series of boyfriends. I had a love affair with Enos, a tech genius. What about you?" I didn't think I should talk about his death to Tim, who looked close to death.

"Their noise goes in random spurts and that drives me crazy. Excuse me for bitching. Joey Chinn was a lovely boy, and he had me thinking white picket fences. He moved in, and he had better taste than I do, so he went about redecorating every room. He was an actor, but after five years with Theater Rhino, the lure of Hollywood fame finally got to him. He got some bit parts in two movies, and last I heard he was in San Diego. He's still a lovely man."

"Were there others?"

"Aren't we supposed to learn from our mistakes? Can you hand me that glass?"

I put the glass with a bendy straw on his chest and he sipped. "I met Maricio Sontag at a fundraiser for the Gay Asian Pacific Alliance, and that kid seduced me. I admit it wasn't just him. I don't like living alone, and I went and fell for him. He moved like a dancer, and we had a few happy years together."

"Did he die?" I was never got comfortable asking that.

"Yes, sadly he died in ninety-eight of Hepatitis B. He didn't even know he had it until the end, and then it was too late."

"I'm so sorry. Damn those doctors!" I joked cynically.

"That's him in those pictures," he said, pointing to the line of silver-framed photos on a shelf behind me.

"How are you doing?"

"This is the result of my second congestive heart failure. I'm hoping I'll be back on my feet in a month or so."

"Is there anything I can do?"

"Social Services through Medicare has someone coming every day. She cleans and makes me lunch and dinner. I'm usually strong enough to make oatmeal in the morning."

"I think all of us want to be loved, and we keep looking," I said, scanning the photos.

"I'm sorry, I need to rest."

"Another time." He took my hand gently and I kissed his cool forehead and left, not sure that he was going to make it. Walking home, I remembered that once I starting playing around, I lost track of him. I thought about what a waste that was. I never had many friends, and I'd lost track of some of them and some had died. But I should have done a better job of staying in touch with them. Friends are more important that sex buddies, and I wasn't sure that I'd have any friends left when my time came.

Chapter Sixteen

Remembering the Dead

Every year for the past twenty years, Tim hosted a dinner on Pride weekend. This one was a little more than a year after my last visit, and Tim had sounded like he'd recovered nicely when we spoke on the phone. His cheeks had good color when he greeted me at the door in slacks and a blue sports coat. It would just the two of us this year and it was his first year sober. I gave him my house gift, a wormwood-framed photo of him in front of a rainbow flag taken at a Pride parade.

"Thank you so much. I remember that day," he said gleefully. We hugged and he motioned me to the dining room where the table was set with his best china, fine crystal, and the silver his mother was given as a wedding present. Two blush roses in a square crystal vase sat in the center of the table. Fog was creeping down Twin Peaks like marshmallows.

As we watched the Pride parade on his new stereo TV, the announcer, his voice coarse from yelling, reminded his listeners that it was second largest public event in the state. Skipping alcohol, Tim had made a punch of fruit juice and ginger ale that I sipped while watching the parade. My heart swelled seeing so many people that cared about people like me that kept passing by and didn't stop. I'd never dreamed there could be so many of us.

While he took the roasted chicken out of the oven, I tossed a salad of various lettuces, shaved carrots, little green onions, and water chestnuts with extra-virgin olive oil and balsamic vinegar. The potato soufflé was one that Tim made every year from a recipe he got from the chef at Boulevard. That went on the hotplate on the table. The fragrant bird, its skin crisp and golden, went next to it and a bone-handled carving knife and matching fork laid out on a crisp napkin.

Tim cut a generous slice of breast and carried it with the knife and fork sideways to a plate and slid it off. A thigh and drumstick were cut with the same precision and carried the same way to another plate. It gave off a butter-burnt skin and sage bouquet that was tantalizing, and my mouth began to water.

"You like white meat or dark?" he asked, wiping his greasy hand on the kitchen towel he kept draped over this shoulder.

"Dark, thanks."

He handed the plate to me and then a large spoon for the soufflé. I used it to scoop out a good portion and leaned over and dropped the gooey mass onto his plate. I did the same with mine. "I'm saving the salad for last," he said.

I didn't know if one should talk about sobriety with alcoholics. Enos' death was on my mind, so I said little as we ate. The meal was much better than the last one, and I thanked him for another splendid meal. I offered the do the dishes, but Tim said he'd do them later and asked me to stay because he wanted to talk to me about Enos. I wasn't sure where that would lead, but he'd been so helpful when I got to town, so I settled in the arm chair while he sat uneasily opposite me on the sectional. A bowl of rainbow M&Ms and the latest issue of the *Advocate* sat between us on the coffee table.

Tim began, "I've known you since you stepped off the bus, and we've had our differences, but I thought I knew you pretty well."

EAT, SLEEP, LOVE

"You were a life-saver."

"I don't understand what you saw in Enos. He wasn't like any of the men you dragged to my parties."

"You are too kind," I said sarcastically.

"I'm sure they were nice men, but Enos?"

"I never thought I'd ever know a PhD in physics from Stanford who started his own company."

"I didn't know he started his own company." His tone meant that Enos owning his own company made him more important.

"He'd also led a life I'd never imagined before meeting him. When you grow up poor, someone who has a condo in Chelsea and a summer home down the beach from Calvin Kline on Fire Island Pines is a big deal."

"You said something about him being duped on the phone."

"What Enos did was ridiculous."

"I want every detail." His eyes grew wide, and I imagined introducing himself to Calvin Kline as giddy as a school girl.

"A gay Puerto Rican named Adam Gonzalez sweet-talked him into giving a series of extravagant parties, the kind where everything has to be the most expensive available. They wrecked his home every time, and the beach was littered with condoms and tubes of KY. They must have been some parties."

"I'm sure you liked the beach part."

"I never did outdoor sex, but if you had bothered to ask me, you would have known."

"How could I possibly keep up with you zipping from one fuck to the next?"

"You had a good job and you're living pretty nice on your pension, but you'll never know what it was like when I wasn't sure Pops' catch would be enough to pay Mr. Giametti the money he owed for rent 'cause he felt ol' man Giametti was a mean sonavabitch. Some days all I ate were the corn flakes that we got in big boxes at Mr. Orson's store. I learned how to write real small because at the beginning of the school year, I got a spiral notebook that had to last the entire year. If I used a fine point pen, I could get a whole report in half a page. We couldn't afford drawing paper, so I made a drawing of waves on toilet paper, but when I left it out overnight, the fog dissolved it. My clothes were handed down by some rich guy who donated them to St. Vincent for the rummage sale. When he shopped, Pops guessed my size and bought what he thought were the best amount of clothing for the money. So I had to roll up the pant legs and stuff shirttails just to look half-way decent. Kids got on me at school for looking like a dork."

"I had no idea you were that poor, dear thing."

"We ate a lot of fish and crab, whatever was in season but only when it was in season. Pops was a lousy shopper, so instead of fresh vegetables he bought huge cans of green beans. If Pops didn't come home, I'd eat the sandwich someone left on a plate at the café. Mrs. Bianchi and her daughter were very nice. Some days they had left-over soup for me."

"He doesn't sound like the nicest father." He swatted an annoying fly.

"The only nice thing about the house was the yard, so I grew radishes, squash, zucchini, Brussels sprouts, and spices like basil. One year, I grew tomatoes, but they don't grow well on the coast, so I stole a sausage from Mr. Orson's and made pizzas. They were sort of pizza because I used bread, but I was so hungry for pizza that the kids at school ate all the time that I thought mine were mighty tasty."

"You said Enos turned you on to food."

"No, he turned me on to cooking food, how to prepare food that brings out its essence. He was so fussy when he lived in Chelsea that he went all the way to a store way uptown just to buy eggs. How could a genius be so stupid?"

"You don't strike me as the jealous type, but you complained about one of his boyfriends."

"Jealousy is the worst. Once it gets its shark teeth in me, it never lets go. It wasn't a boyfriend; it was a pro baseball player that Enos met the summer he rented a summer home

in Provincetown that he tried to make his boyfriend. He even
went back the next summer, but the guy still didn't want to be
his boyfriend."

"Why complain if he wasn't his boyfriend?"

"The motherfucker got traded three times!"

He broke out laughing.

"How would you feel about someone who got traded three
times?"

"I have good reason to believe I will never date a pro-
baseball player, but you weren't trying to date him," he said,
laughing.

"Don't you see what that meant about what he thought of
me?"

"Would you have felt better if he tried to date say a star
pitcher? They have pitchers in baseball, don't they?"

"I wasn't on a par with someone who got traded three
times."

"Poor child. I can't believe someone who's taken home half
the men in town would be happier if it was a star pitcher. What
drugs are you on?"

"Don't you see where that left me?" I took a handful of
cashews and debated what to do with them.

"Little Charlie McKey thinks his boyfriend should have
better taste in men." He lit his one cigarette for the day, a Kent.

"Stop calling me little."

"What's that look?" he asked.

"I found a key when I was going through Pops' things and
that began the biggest search in my life."

Pops died at eighty-one of a heart attack, and the autopsy that
I requested showed there was cirrhosis in his liver. I scattered
his ashes at the slip where he kept his boat, alone because the
men from the bar were long gone. I put off going through his
things for as long as I could because there was so much of it,
mostly in boxes stacked on top of each other in a shed behind
his office I'd never seen. I went through random boxes and

most of what I found were years of court records for two of the fishing fleets, decades of letters on yellowing paper and others with everything he took apart but was never able to put back together—batteries, springs, metal casings. It took renting a truck with a big bed to haul the boxes to a land fill. I thought after that, his office would be a piece of cake, but he was hoarder and he was ingenious in the way he could cram things into small spaces. I had to pry some stuff out with pliers, like the rolled-up maps of the bay with markings for all of the underwater features and the lines of the tide movements. Another was a banner from an army unit. He'd never said he'd served in the army so it could have been a gift.

The most intriguing thing was a key in the pen holder in the big drawer of a desk that must have been more than a hundred years old. It was the kind of key that opened the locker where I used to stow my bag in the airline transfer terminals in downtown San Francisco, but there must be thousands of those lockers in bus stations and airports all over the world. Even if I lived a long time, I wouldn't have time to try every lock in those terminal and stations, so I put the key in the little paper box on my desk, where I used to keep phone numbers, and forgot about it.

It must have been the Universe that got me wanting to see what was in the locker, because I woke one day and felt I could find the locker. After looking at maps for the Greyhound, Trailways, and Jefferson bus routes as well as the number of Amtrak stations, I threw up my hands in despair. There was no way I could get to all of them, and I didn't know why I thought I could; that was downright stupid. Late one night months later, I was watching *Murder on the Orient Express*, and my frazzled mind connected the train and the detective and key, and I thought, why not hire a detective to find the locker?

That was easier said than done. I stumbled around trying to find a simple list of detectives, discovering that they went by names that mask what they do, for obvious reasons; if you're trying to uncover something about someone, you don't want them to know. Businesses advertising home security wanted to sell me all kinds of shit to protect my house, or so they claimed. Most that were more clearly identified as what I would call a spy were hired to follow husbands their wives suspected were cheating. I finally found someone who claimed he could find the locker. He was not someone I'd invite to brunch, and I would have been uncomfortable being seen with him in public. He was pudgy man with the face of a Doberman pinscher who kept an unlit cigar hanging from the corner of his mouth. Nevertheless, he was dogged. I don't know how he did it, and didn't want to know, but after a year, he found the locker in a bank of lockers in the Greyhound Terminal in Portland. He said he got there just in time, because if he'd come a week later, the terminal would be a hole in the ground that would eventually become a twelve-story office building. The bank of lockers was going to be moved to another location. I told him not to open it, so he mailed me the key, but he forgot to tell me the new location if he knew it. Fuck! One minute I was cheering the guy for finding the locker I thought no one could find, and the next I was pissed at him for not finding out where the goddamned locker went.

It was a long trip to Portland, so I put off going. In the middle of the night I sat bolt upright. What if that new location was going to be destroyed? I had a sudden urge to find the locker in the new location.

Fortunately, a buddy I knew, Dan Pillars, was an artist who lived in Portland. Dan agreed to host me, so I drove to Portland. I was bushed when I got to Dan's tidy bungalow and slept most of the next day on his couch. I was so eager to find the locker, I demurred when Dan asked if I wanted to get in his sling. But that didn't stop him from being quite the sleuth. He found the locker in Portland's new transit center that connects Amtrak, all the buses, and the city's new light rail. I was jazzed. We hopped in his car and Dan drove like a maniac to the terminal, where he took me to the bank of lockers.

"What's that? Dan asked as I extracted my prize, a battered metal box the size of a tackle box from the steel locker.

"I dunno. There aren't any markings and it's locked."

"Should we smash it open?" he asked excitedly.

"I think it's better if I take it home. Who knows what's in it."

"But what if there's a treasure map inside?'

"I think we can be damn sure there's no treasure map," I said jokingly.

Why would Pops park the box in Portland? That was the question I kept asking myself when I got home. Did he even know what was in it? If he needed safe keeping, why would he put it hundreds of miles away? Perhaps whatever was in it was so odious that he wanted it as far away as possible. But if it was odious, why would he bother keeping it? Those were questions that would never be answered.

Opening the box required tools that were my nemesis, so I kept putting it off. I finally decided I had to find out what was inside. I would get a locksmith to unlock it. That was much easier than finding the detective. Once he opened it with his tools that looked like a jeweler's tools, he left. With Pooch at my feet watching, I cautiously opened it with my hand using the other as a guard in case something jumped out when I opened it. Inside I found what felt like papers that had been carefully wrapped in purple velvet. They felt brittle, so I carefully peeled back the outermost corner of the wrapping. I could see that it was hand-written letters that had been neatly stacked on top of each other so well that, if I had used a ruler, they wouldn't have been more perfectly aligned. They were tied with blue cord, like a gift to be presented to a king or queen.

I didn't want to rip anything, so I used my sharpest kitchen knife to slice through the cord. Corner by corner, I opened the first letter. It was a handwritten letter in English but even when I looked a second time, I didn't recognize some words. I opened the next letter in the stack, hoping it would be in clear English, but it was totally incomprehensible. They were written in English script, but I didn't recognize any of them or their arrangements. I put them back and shut the case. I'd been fussing over it for weeks, and I needed a break.

Several weeks later, Richard Street saw the box on top of the bookcase in the bedroom where I'd put it to keep it out of reach of Pooch. He asked what it was, and I took it down and showed him the wrapped stack of letters.

"Have you looked at them?" he asked.

"I looked at two, and one was a little better than the other, but it's English with weird words. I can only guess what the other's written in."

"Can I see one? I'll be careful."

I carefully unwrapped them and gingerly withdrew the top one without disturbing the others.

He went to get his classes and, greasy from play, he washed his hands before coming back and examining the letter that I'd flattened on the top of the bedside table.

"Do you know what this is?" he asked.

"Like I said, it has some weird English words."

"Do you know Ed Ogglethorpe?"

"Sure, I played with him at the baths years ago. What's he up to?"

"Did you know he's a language specialist at Stanford?"

"I knew he was a professor of something."

"You were too busy playing around to ask him," he said sarcastically, "but he's a leading authority on languages. He should see all of them."

Professor Ogglethorpe's office in Margaret Jacks Hall looked like a library. Every square inch of its walls was covered by books—big, small, and odd-sized. Some were upright, others on their side. There were scrolls. He sat behind a modest desk, with an unlit pipe and wireless glasses. He wore a Harris Tweed jacket and an open shirt. When he got up, I saw he was wearing jeans and sneakers.

"Hi, Charlie. Is that the box you want me to see? Have a seat."

I put the box on the desk and sat in front of it. "My father stored it in a locker in Portland, but I haven't a clue why."

"You said there were letters that you couldn't read and one that was completely foreign."

"That's right. Richard said you might be able to tell me what they are."

"How's Richard? He's a lot of fun, but I had a hard time keeping up with him."

"He's fine." I handed him the wrapped letters.

He put on a pair of white cotton gloves and slowly opened the stack and laid them out on velvet. He picked up the first and read the letter. He carefully put it down and opened the next like a surgeon. His eyes were wide as he scrutinized it.

"Would you mind if I keep these? It would just be a couple days or maybe a week. What you have here is most unusual and I will need that much time to fully ascertain their meaning," he said, sounding like this was a major discovery.

"You think it's bad?" I never thoughts Pops did anything illegal, but he wasn't home much, so what did I know?

"Quite the contrary. There's the bell, I have to be off to class. Richard can give me your number, and I'll call as soon as I can tell you what you have."

He dashed off.

He didn't give me any comfort; unusual can mean a lot of things, most of them bad. Riding back on the train, the word kept repeating in my brain. By the time I got home, I had only enough mental energy to take Pooch to the park.

The anticipation had been eating me for a week as I waited outside Professor Oglethorpe's office. I'd been there maybe five minutes when he came bounding down the hall. "Come take a seat. What do you know about your grandfather or it could be your great-grandfather?" he asked as he sat behind the desk, acting like knowing about my grandfather or great-grandfather was essential.

"I barely knew my relatives. Pops never talked about his and none of them came to my mother's funeral."

"I'm sorry for your mother. But you know nothing of anyone before your father? I know how some families don't get along, so are your sure he never said something in passing? Just dropped a name?"

"I don't know if he liked them or not, but he never mentioned them when I was in the room. Why do you ask?"

"You have something very special in these letters. At some time in the future, if you would be so kind to donate them to Stanford, I can say with confidence that they will give a future graduate student enough for a sound book, possibly two. "

"What are they?" I asked, beside myself with anticipation.

"They are love letters between two men. We never see letters like this that are that old. The one you said was incomprehensible was written by someone who lived very likely in Orkney, a Scottish Island, because he was writing in an ancient language called Norn. I'm guessing because in those days, letters got read by the local magistrates, he didn't want them to know what he'd written. The other steals some of Robert Burns' lines, so he likely lived around Edinburgh in Scotland."

"You say they're love letters between two men? How old are they?" My heart was beating overtime.

"One of them is very likely a distant relative of yours, and the way they talk about love is clearly early nineteenth century. They use different words than the ones we usually use when we're talking about love, and some of them are quite explicit. Those men were in love and they did it when they got together," he said with a knowing smile.

"Do you know which one is my relative? Did he wear kilts?" I know it sounded silly, but I had to know which one so I could look him and his family up on the Internet

"You're getting ahead of yourself. Your letters are priceless. To fully understand who wrote them and the exact wording of each one is going to take several years of work by a top mind." He waved his hand over the stack as if he could protect them by doing that.

I thanked him profusely and left the letters with him, hoping he'd tell me what they were as soon as possible because I had to know who he was. I came back with a strange new warm feeling about my McKey family.

Tim refreshed my tea as I told him about the love letters, and how one of the writers might be a relative.

"That's lovely, but how do you know they're real?"

"The head of the linguistics department at Stanford authenticated them."

"That's what I like about you. You don't mess with the small stuff."

Knowing I might have a gay ancestor, I never slept better than I did that night.

Chapter Seventeen

"Touch me, remind me who I am."
—Stanley Kunitz, poet

2013

I didn't know the brash Charlie who crossed the bridge, a kid I knew a long time ago. It's said that experience hardens you but it molded me. Today, I am the accumulation of everything stolen from the men I played with and lungs of San Francisco air. The circuits in my brain run on lines formed in my first years out, pissed at my disappointments and wallowing in swells of joy. The loss of the only man I loved eats away, and I touch the wound lovingly.

When I heard the fishermen complain about how much better their lives were when they young, I said I wasn't going to complain; my life was too good for that. When I was younger, it was easier to be alive, but I tried to see each day for what it was. I learned from each setback and grew with the discoveries, like being capable of loving a man. I was saner with the tricky emotional issues than the adults in my life had been with theirs because I knew happiness. I like to think what trails me is not a cloud of dust but a string of moments that made my life endlessly fascinating.

Living is a packing on of experience, dressing the tree, and while some episodes of my life weren't pretty, I've had a challenging and ultimately satisfying life and I am grateful for all of the people who made it so.

I think the first years I spent in San Francisco will likely go down in history as one of the most spectacularly good years for gay men; they were for me. They were magical years when I and the men of my generation in San Francisco were basically given a clean slate to write our own rules. Few of us had been public with our sexuality, so we made it up as we went along. My most common way of meeting someone in the early years was sharing coming out stories, and they told me we came from a thousand different backgrounds. Each of them had molded a life that fit them. Some came from super-restrictive parts of the country; especially the South, where fundamentalist religion held sway over the way the general populace thought about sex. Others came from less restrictive parts of the country, but all of them said they could never be fully out about their sexuality there.

San Francisco was our beacon of hope, my first chance to live free. The only way that men found out about the city was through friends who'd either been to San Francisco or knew someone who'd been there. They didn't have to be there long, some were just service men passing through on their way home from war, but even in the short time they were there, they knew that San Francisco was unlike anywhere else. For many of the ones I knew, it was just what they'd been looking for but never found. I remember walking down the street and thinking, "This can't actually be happening. No place like this can possibly exist." Clerks in town whom I expected would be straight were gay; even a few cops were openly gay.

That freedom was too much for some men. I think they came to San Francisco expecting some kind of hassle-free nirvana, but freedom comes with responsibility and they couldn't handle it. I suppose that's why some people need churches; they need structure and someone telling them right from wrong. I had to do that for myself.

The other thing that was special about those days, and is now gone, was my optimism. Every man's coming out story invariably included talking about how we were strong enough to change the way Americans thought about things and not just our sexuality. Some of the teachers I dated saw us changing the way schools educate kids, and others who'd marched against the war in Vietnam were convinced that once the war was over, there would never be another war. I just wanted Nixon gone. I knew that was asking a lot, but since I could pretty much do anything I wanted to do in San Francisco, I thought everyone else could do it too.

Staring at people was considered bad taste. The first time a man stared at me, I freaked. He wasn't being sly and he didn't want something from me, he was just acknowledging me. Who did that? I got over being freaked and so after that, someone staring at me made me feel worthy as a human being. I can't come up with enough superlatives to describe those years; they were magical. As a kid, I thought I'd grow up and be just as stuck in life as everyone around me was. But in San Francisco, the air screamed, "Get out there and discover who you really are!"

That took guts! I know for me I couldn't have become the person I am today, had it not been for San Francisco in those years. They almost made me want to believe there was a God.

I saw that being eroded. Once there were a lot of pickups on the street, I knew the pendulum was swinging the other way. Ever since then, I've tried not to be a cynic, but it's harder and harder to do that.

When I talked about it with my friends, they said they also noticed the change. The worst part of the change was a new modesty. My first gyms had gang showers. I saw men showering around me, and no one seemed embarrassed about being naked in the locker room. Men started covering with a towel when they went from the locker room to the shower. Soon the gyms had individual showers so you couldn't see the other men. Men who were proud of their bodies and wanted to let others see what they'd done with their bodies were replaced with prim schoolmarms. It felt like an army of Bible-thumpers had descended on the city and declared martial law.

Men I admired at the gym for their finely developed bodies and healthy lives died of AIDS as fast as the men who drank too much and led desultory lives. I expected there was cosmic justice, but it failed me. I thought the Universe that had provided me with so many wonderful opportunities would look after the friends who taught me how to be gay, but it failed me. I thought that modern medicine that developed cures for polio and most forms of VD would step up and come up with either a cure or a vaccine so my friends and lovers would live, but it failed me.

Even when I had more and more days of being alive in my back pocket I couldn't face the friends who were going to be an obituary in the BAR. I felt I had failed them and failed as a human being. I had to do whatever I could to stop AIDS, but I couldn't face delivering another meal to a homebound man or guide another discussion group of men who were dealing with AIDS. I didn't feel guilty for surviving; I felt inadequate for not being able to save the thousands of men I loved.

 I stopped counting the friends who died after Tom and Ted died of AIDS complications within weeks of each other. I'd never known men with so much joy in their hearts, who provided holiday cheer for home-bound men without families and struck up friendships spontaneously and spread their joy. They can never be replaced.

My buddy Rusty's art that was about to be shown in a major gallery will never be seen because he died two weeks after being diagnosed and he never had time to organize it. Another buddy, Freddie, his musical promise would never be realized because he died too young. The only man I loved, Enos, was gone. You can't destroy more than half of a community and expect it will ever come back.

The band of beautiful brothers, me included, that had paraded proudly through the early '70s with the songs "Over the Rainbow" and "San Francisco" in our hearts dispersed, some to the bathhouse in the sky and others went back to where they came from. I was left with echoing ghosts of the past. I had no future, and thinking about the past sent me deeper into depression.

The city that had once had been as lush as the flowerbeds at the Conservatory of Flowers was a desolate landscape. The men in my life had been ripped from me, and I kept thinking, "What if I had just…"

Chapter Eighteen

A Man and His Dog

2011

I wanted a standard poodle companion to accompany me in my life as a single man. My early searches online were surreal ventures in the world of canine royalty that peddles piddle pads. I was a lowly peasant barely granted permission to sniff their butt, much less take a jewel from the crown without paying homage to enough blue ribbons to sink the *Titanic*. I just wanted a four-legged pal to hang with, and a breeder's address in the far Delta sounded like it might be real people who raised dogs.

Her rundown wooden home at the end of dirt road looked like Dorothy's after it had collapsed to earth. I opened the front door, and I was stopped dead at the door by the dogshit and piss fumes. I covered my burning eyes and nose and stepped cautiously into next the room, and like the electric bulb Christ in the St. Vincent's Christmas manger, two large brown eyes glowed at the bottom of a cardboard crate. I picked him up. When my cheek got a tongue wash, I knew he was the one. I paid the breeder and wrapped the god in an old army blanket and set him on the seat beside me in my new Audi, his large brown eyes already fixed on the mark he was going to bend to his curly haired will.

Crossing the bridge, the still unnamed pup threw up, but I came prepared with paper towels. When we got to the flat, he was as good as new, but the car looked like teenagers had just had sex in it at a drive-in. I put him at the bottom step, but he was not as tall as the step. He tried to climb and after falling back, he twisted around and gamely tried his best and failed a second time. I ended up carrying him upstairs. I was the only living thing he cared about. As soon as he knew his name, the same as my last dog, Pooch, he came when called. I thought he did far better than the other fuzzballs in his class at the ASPCA's training program as they went through their paces on the polished high school gym floor.

A few weeks later, I was visiting Jesse Carrol, an old friend from the baths, at his home in Forestville. We'd already caught up on our lives over the crab bisque course, and I was watching a squirrel cross a power line like a high wire artist, when Jessie returned with a ceramic platter with thick egg salad sandwiches and a fat dill pickle.

"I hear you did a sex manual."

"I figured since I'm not going to be around forever, who better? I want the young kids to know how we did it because they don't seem that interested in sex."

"It must be encyclopedic," he said, rolling his eyes.

"You are too kind. It's just important stuff like get everything done before he walks in the door and thank him when you're done," I said half-joking.

"I swear to God, it must have been one of the men I played with in Columbus who came up with those little individual jars of Crisco. I'd go through half a roll of paper towels."

"If it weren't for Dawn detergent, I never would have gotten the smell of Crisco and poppers out of my sheets."

"I can't tell you how many times they walked out without saying a word. The cute ones missed out when they were handing out brains."

"San Francisco isn't the city I fell in love with," I said. I heard a sadness in my voice I hadn't heard before.

"Why don't you come here? I can't believe it took me so long and I can hook you up with someone."

The next day Jesse introduced me to Julie Morris, an older gay Realtor who, in a good blue suit, was standing next to his Mercedes SUV. Over the next two weeks he showed me properties in Sonoma County that he said were in my price range. Two homes among the more than twenty homes I looked at as Julie drove me around the county stood out for different reasons. The worst in Healdsburg had a vast space with a high ceiling in the middle. I would have felt like the sole survivor in the hold of a slave ship if I had used it as a living room.

The home that I bought on county land was on a lane with blackberry brambles on one side and a view of a valley on the other. It had a good-sized garden, and an out building. I had no need for an out building, but I liked the idea of one. It was a little over an hour from the city, so when I needed a museum fix, I could zip down to the city and be back in time for dinner. The house was well put together by able craftsmen, but the kitchen with painted farm animal tiles and the strangely arranged sinks and appliances were designed for someone who must have liked folk art but detested preparing meals that had become my life blood. By renovating every property that I co-owned or rented, I'd earned enough merit badges to make this a beauty with tons of potential my own.

The bedroom had a spectacular view of the valley and further mountains, and the dining room opened to a patio where I would have my morning tea. The property was fenced, so all I had to do was open the door and bingo Pooch was walked.

Jesse turned me on to a contractor who he said was a must for every homeowner. I wished he'd told me about him when I thought I could do it on my own that invariably turned into nightmares. Joe, a burly former cop, was a competent electrician and plumber, and while our tastes were drastically different, without grumbling, he laid my choice of tile on the expanded kitchen floor and my chosen backsplash behind the new farmhouse sink. I have a brown thumb, so I neglected the garden. I had no use for the shed.

I started cooking for myself after Enos died. With the folks in Sonoma County taking agriculture seriously, I had to change everything I ate; no more steaks and rich desserts. An Asian man sold sweet little strawberries at his roadside stand, and a local market had just-off-the-boat seafood and good local produce, so I kept my larder stocked with the freshest. The redwoods surrounding my home made it feel like a gnome's cottage. Being nestled there amongst them gave me a layer of fairy tale padding between the hope of for a better world in Sonoma County and the loss of my friends in the city. By avoiding the memorial services for my buddies that were within me but were not at the service, I'd gotten through the epidemic HIV-positive and I was very much alive.

Being around the aging hippies at the farmers markets and on the streets in town reminded me of the weekends that a gang of us went to the Russian River. The group always changed because new men showed up all the time, and there had to be someone who owned a car or a pickup with enough gas to get us to Guerneville. We camped overnight and I slept in a sleeping bag on flat land near the river's music. Inside the fairy ring of redwoods, there was just enough light to light the Coleman cook stove.

We sucked dicks to confirm our overnight friendships; it wasn't I-want-a-boyfriend sex; they were like the handshakes Hopalong Cassidy used to confirm a cowboy agreement. Everyone loved food, so one of the magical moments was dusk, when the man who'd taken responsibility for preparing dinner worked his culinary magic in a skillet with the food we bought along the road. The men came from all corners of the country, so one weekend it was Cajun, another it was Pennsylvania Dutch, and another was seafood. I appropriated the coping of men's coming out stories told over dinner and used them in making my new life as a gay man.

I retraced my steps in Guerneville on an overcast April day to see if the mecca for the dispossessed, who believed their salvation was smoking dope and being as close to the earth as possible, was still there. The theater marquee looked like on old man waiting for a bus and the theater was dark. Some storefronts were empty and others had changed from floor-to-ceiling rainbow T-shirts and jock straps to salsa and corn chips. The gray bank that could have been a bank in any small town was boarded up like a wounded warrior. I drove Cazadero Road, where I used to see men camped out in tents along it. If they waved, I stopped and we'd share a joint. While sipping tequila sunrises, we had get-to-know-you sex before I left.

The tents and the men were gone, but the rolling land brought back fairy tale memories of how glad I was to be alive with a thousand friends, because they came to San Francisco when I did. If a decent, upright citizen had told me then that Jesus didn't approve of my life, I would have told him my Jesus wore jeans and had a big dick.

As I stood on the bridge and looked out at Guerneville, I looked back on my career as a player. I'd already hung up my spurs and found I didn't miss sex as much as I'd expected. My career spanned almost thirty years, playing every day the first decade, and that adds up to making close, intimate connections with more than a thousand unique queer personalities.

Beneath the bridge, powerful shoulders glided a canoe in perfect harmony with the river, a harmony that reminded me of the harmony of having sex, the joy of feeling his warmth against my flesh, and the feeling of acceptance when I was lying next to him and remembering the energy that we exchanged because sex had been my way of getting held by a man, a stark realization a few years ago.

The canoe was long gone when I remembered what I put into every date with a man. There was the physical energy I put into cleaning the apartment and then making the play area ready, getting out the ladder to hang the sling and hanging it, last-minute running to the dirty book store for a fresh bottle of poppers or to Safeway for a can of Crisco. There was also the time I spent mentally preparing myself for the date to make sure I was in the right frame of mind; I could spend hours in the shower. All of it was enough to kill a horse, but I would do it again in a flash.

The Rainbow Cattle Company in Guerneville had the same warm vibe as the bar in the city of the same name. In both, if I didn't know everyone, I still felt at home. The men in the city in their jeans and flannel shirts were comfortable with their masculinity, and all of them had mustaches and many had beards as they talked about politics. The hippie spirit survived in the county. The men there, who also had facial hair given any excuse, would dress up and then get in the middle of the road in a dowdy dress that a well-formed woman wore to her daughter's wedding, with Barbara Bush pearls and Mardi Gras beads, proclaiming, "I'm here. I'm queer, get used to it, motherfuckers!"

As I entered, I wondered if there might be a way that I could have what I liked about sex dates, the merging of bodies and souls, without the hassles of cleaning out before the date and cleaning up after it. Then I decided that was asking a lot for a man of seventy. In the bar's mellow darkness, bearded men in sleeveless flannel shirts and cargo shorts talked quietly beneath a beer sign. I sat alone at the mahogany bar with a carved-wood mirror. I asked the bearded barkeep with gold earring for a glass of sparkling water.

"Don't I know you?" he asked cheerfully.

We chatted and discovered that we'd had sex when he lived in the city, and I vaguely remembered him. But talking with him conjured memories of the scent of Herbal Essence shampoo in the beard of a bear that I had played with. I'd already shared my coming out story with him. The barkeep was near the end of his when the door opened and flooded the bar with low October light. A tall shadow walked up to the bar, leaned over, and planted a wet one on the barkeep's furry lips.

"Hey, Artimus! Where you been?" the barkeep asked.

"I've been in Santa Ana getting my massage certificate, 'cause my aunt lives there, and she did my laundry."

"Well, don't you look like one healthy sonavabitch. What can I getcha?" the barkeep asked.

"I'll have what he's having." Artimus checked to see if it was OK with me and I nodded assent.

"So, it's no more Bailey's White Russians for the lad?" The barkeep turned and pulled a pitcher from the sink of ice below the bar and filled a narrow glass on the bar.

"If anyone asks about a masseur, here's my card." He wiped the card across his sleeve and handed it to the barkeep.

I turned to a tall man with cropped blond hair, clear blue eyes, and a rosy-cheeked face. "I love massage, but since I got here, I haven't found anyone," I told him.

He was guarded but his smile was genuine. "Would you be interested in me massaging you? Call me Arti." He gave me his card.

"I'd like that very much." I wrote my address on it and handed it to him.

When I left the bar, I laughed because I was instantly attracted to Arti. He had none of the annoying traits that I associated with gay men.

Arti arrived at my new home on time in shorts and a tank top with his table in a cloth case slung over his shoulder. He set it down long enough to wrap me in his arms for a good hug, and he then looked around the room. He nodded at an open space between the couch and the wall, and I nodded back. Once the table covering was removed, folded, and put on a chair, he set up the table in the space. With the legs stable and the joints snapped shut, he covered the top with a brown flannel fitted sheet and added a similarly covered Tootsie Roll-shaped pillow. I stripped and sat on the edge of the table.

"Do you mind if I toke? Would you like some?" he asked.

"What can I say?"

He lit his blown-glass pipe, took a hit, and passed it to me. We did two hits each, and I then lay face down on the table with my head in the cradle when the dope began taking effect.

Arti, in gym shorts, strapped a container of lotion to his waist. "My massages are not sexual. Do you have any special areas that need attention?"

"I store tension in my lower back."

He placed one of his warmed hands near the top of my spine and another at the bottom of my spine on the arc of my butt. That got the energy moving and he began one of the most intimate ninety minutes I had ever had. While he was massaging my back, I gently rested my hand on his leg. He stopped the massage, saying, "When you touch me, it's no longer my massage."

"But I …"

"I'm looking for a boyfriend my age."

He continued the massage, stretching muscles that hadn't moved in years, in a series of sensuous movements and strokes that stripped anxieties off knotted muscles. The only time we broke was when I rolled over so he could do his magic on my other side. I'd worked with some very fine masseurs, but while I hadn't seen one for some time, his felt like one of the best I'd ever had.

He put his hands together and bowed. "Namaste."

I sat on the edge of the table and did the same. "Namaste."

I always took an active part of my massages in the city. Using sounds and motions, I let the masseur know that a particular part of me enjoyed what he was doing to it or to shift his attention elsewhere, always feeding the energy that he was putting into me with his hands back into him with mine. Massage had always been a mutual exchange, and touching him made me feel complete with him. We always had more than just a "California finish." I thought the only way I could stop touching Arti was to give my power to him. That's what I did at the next massage. Because he knew my body, his second massage was even better than the first.

When Arti said he was looking for a place, I offered him the shed if he'd do the work to make it livable.

"Thank you. I've done a lot or carpentry and I'd love to do that."

A couple months later, I noticed a pick-up parked overnight at the shed and asked Arti the next day about the truck. He confessed he had a boyfriend, Tom. Tom was a handyman, so few days later after checking with Arti to see if it was OK with him, I asked Tom to fix a window. When he came to the house, his smile and good looks in the old days would have been all that I needed to talk him into having sex, but now, having a loving couple on the property, made the land that I lived on feel like it was home to a family. For Arti's birthday, I took Arti and Tom out to dinner.

 Arti discovered my hot spots and became exceptionally good at using them to take me to states of bliss. When he stopped working on a spot and went on to another, I missed the sublime joy of his touch at that spot. But I also felt that in that moment that he'd given me the same level of pleasure I experienced when I was having sex. Arti was so good at taking care of me that I began trusting him, but I realized that by giving my power back to him, I was still controlling what happened. Was there a step beyond that? Could I stop controlling? What would happen to me if I did? Decades-old fears rose up like slow-moving rivers of lava.

I didn't know how Arti did it, but the sensations that swept me away were better, sweeter, and more intimate than any sex I had ever had. The feeling lifted me up to a plane of peace, a cloud of sublime ease with me. I didn't know that my life had been an ongoing struggle between the part that was out to live the best life I could lead as a gay man and a native part that needed connection with itself. I wondered if that was true with everyone; perhaps it's the state that yogis work years to attain.

Arti took me to a place I never imagined. I wasn't sure I was ever capturing it adequately in the words I wrote in my journal, but it was a profound sense of who I was as a human being in some greater sense of being. Fisting had been about experimenting with ways of finding the ultimate method of being touched, but Arti took me to a fifth dimension, something I didn't know even existed. When I was with Arti, I responded the same way I responded when I was twenty-three. I even had fuck farts when I was completely relaxed. Just inside the ring of a butthole, there's a space; I know, my hands had been in many of them. That space collects gas produced in our stomachs and bowels. When the ring is relaxed, the gas slips out. Those escaping bubbles of air told Arti he'd relaxed me.

Pops had been erratic, and I never knew his mood and seldom his intention. I barricaded myself so I could be as prepared as I could be, ready for whatever his state of mind on any given day. I thought that when I came out that I had dropped those shields, the ways I protected myself growing up, and all the little ways that kept me from being hurt, but I hadn't. They were deeply ingrained, and I would live with them the rest of my life. What Arti did was to make it so safe that I could get past my devils. They didn't go away, but Arti got me to a place where I let them sit. That gave new dimensions to the meaning of being touched.

When Tom and Ted talked about oneself, I thought the idea was novel, but I never took the time to understand it and then I forgot about it. Arti never talked about his intentions, but I sensed he was trying to get me to a state of oneness.

Arti had been working on me for a year when he got me to where my barriers existed. He got me to where I was floating in a sea of clear unlike anything I'd ever felt. With nothing protecting me, vulnerable from all sides, I felt strong but a different kind of strong, my strong. I was the Charlie that had always been there, but over time, layer upon layer of experience and layer upon layer of hurt have been piled on it, so I didn't know it was there. I don't know if Arti was looking to get me to a oneness or his practice was getting his clients as relaxed as possible, but he took me to a place where I was pure and strong.

Fisting had taught me to relax the base muscles in my butt that were attached to a host of other muscles. When my butt and lower back muscles were relaxed, my entire body smoothed out. I thought that was the ultimate state of relaxation. Arti's relaxation felt purer than the relaxation I remembered from fisting; it was another level, a serene level and it was mine. Guided by Arti, I reached a state where I had a force in me that I had never felt. I was grateful for experiencing that at this time in my life, when things were supposed to slow down. Arti's massages gave me a new vibrant sense of living.

Part of the difference between massage and sex was simple hygiene, but my connection with Arti went beyond that. It was also spiritual. Being spiritual was something I went along with originally, when my hippie friends talked about it without knowing what it was. On Arti's table, I merged with life in a profoundly intimate way, every fiber of me was alive and joined to every living thing in the Universe, a natural connection to something immense, so immense I would never fully understand. But I accepted its immensity, and I was grateful to be part of it.

I loved Enos. Ours was a furious love. A love of that instant, a fire quickly kindled. It overwhelmed me. I'd never felt the connection to Enos that I felt with anyone else, and for a time, I thought that he and I would be inseparable for the rest of our lives. Our love was manic and beautiful; it was love of men in the middle of an epidemic.

What I felt for Arti was a different love, a gentle love that lingered in silence. Was that love what I'd been looking for? I didn't know if it was what I'd been looking for because I believe we never know what we want until we have it. Arti and I expressed our love for each other our way. What we had was more than I ever thought I could have, it was magical.

Chapter Nineteen

"The past beats inside me."
—John Banville, novelist

In my heavy terrycloth robe, fresh from a shower, I put the shoebox of photos on my Mission desk and began going through the photos in the box to remind me of what I'd done with my life. The first one I looked at was a color photo of Mom's funeral. The day is overcast and Pops stands with his head bowed at the grave site with specks of freshly turned earth on the heel of his boot. I started crying, so I put it down to make a cup of tea. With my tea on a coaster, I retrieved a pack of photos that Mom took on her trip to Paris. In one, she stands in front of 27 Rue de Fleurus, Gertrude Stein's home, wearing a blue-striped cotton sweater and baggy white pants. In the other, she is waving at the camera from the highly-polished wood deck of a canal boat on the Seine with Notre-Dame in the background. I put those down and took a leak; I'd been putting off looking at the photos of Enos. I came back and pulled out the slender pack of him.

In the first, he's standing in front of a home on Beaver Street that had its Victorian elements lovingly preserved; he looked so sweet. In another, he's showing me his latest invention, which was the size of a bar of soap. I wondered what was it about him that made me fall in love with him? I modeled my role in our relationship on the men that I'd had sex with. This was alarmingly accurate because our relationship ended just like many of theirs did. I couldn't look at any more and put them back.

For old times' sake, before going to sleep, I pulled out the sleeve with the Polaroids taken my first year in town of Castro denizens in my "Robert Mapplethorpe" period. They were all fresh, smiling faces in different places in the city, each guy still amazed that a city like San Francisco existed. When I thought about what they must have looked like at their last Pride parade, gaunt and barely able to stand in some cases, sharp pain pierced me like a dagger. I'd lost almost all my friends. The Polaroids were out of focus, and so was I when I took them because at the time I believed gay men could change the world. When I thought about how sure I was that we were going to change the world, I laughed. But what a beautiful, loving world it would have been had my dreams come true.

I put the Polaroids back so I could mount my pièce de résistance. The treasure I held dearest was a high-resolution black and white 8″ × 10″ photo of me and Arti smiling at each other, holding a 4′ × 4′ piece of knotted fabric and sea shells. Two years before it was taken, we had turned his home into a workshop for our shared passion, reviving the art of macramé.

I slid the photo into the mounting, kissed Arti's cheek, put him and me next to me on the bedside table, and slid beneath the comforter, thanking the Universe that I'd been given a life I never dreamed could be mine.

Author's Note

I knew a time that most gay men will never know because I came out along with thousands of men roughly my age in the early '70s in San Francisco, the first mass coming out in history. It was a magical, once-in-a-lifetime moment in time. With its history of tolerance, San Francisco gave us the freedom to create the first queer community, with no strings attached. Thanks to the middle class that was fed up with apartments and wanted two-car garages and swimming pools, we got some of the choicest real estate in the country to do it in. Every day, something I never expected happened, like an apartment, with its own garden that I'd lusted after, was available the next day. I thought, "Oh my God, is it real?" Sometimes it happened twice, like the day a gay bank opened and the staff at the city's free VD clinic didn't care about my name or address, just the names of the men I'd recently had sex with. I couldn't believe there'd ever be a gay bank or that a VD clinic would be free and it cared about our health. Our whole-hearted optimism and the brotherhood we felt for one another are etched in memory. It was a time that will never come again, and I regret that younger gay men will never experience the exuberance that I felt then just for being able to be a gay man. If Enos dreamed of a nirvana, his nirvana wouldn't have been as perfect as San Francisco was for me. I felt that just being there with my brothers, I was making history. For someone from an inconsequential town, that was huge.

Acknowledgments

They say it takes a village to raise a child; it takes a tribe to write a novel. Michael Samuel kept my spirits up, and he patiently listened to the chapters as I wrote them; I couldn't have written this without him. I also have to thank my son Seth, Rochelle Doble, David Penner, and Trebor Healey who kept me strong and positive through the ordeal; writing a novel is like trying to raise an inconsiderate child. I wouldn't be here if my trainer David Ames, my acupuncturist Alan Scoop, and the able staff at Kaiser who have kept me alive. Special thanks to Don Weise, the finest editor a man could have who wisely showed me how adults write novels. I also want to thank Tony Valenzuela, David Groff, and Ned Bayrd for reading the novel prior to publication. Dan Nicoletta gets my thanks for the use of his photograph on the cover.

I'd be remiss if I didn't acknowledge the inheritances from three of my four parents that have allowed me to be a writer who never worried about paying the rent on time.

About the Author

Chuck Forester was raised in northern Wisconsin and attended Dartmouth and Penn and holds a MCP in city planning and an MFA in poetry. He is the author of the novel *Our Time*. He spent two years in the Peace Corps in Chile with his wife, and his son was born shortly after they arrived in San Francisco in 1971. Chuck worked for three San Francisco mayors before serving as an executive with several nonprofits. He was chairman of the Board of the Human Rights Campaign Committee, now the Human Rights Campaign (HRC), and he led the effort that raised $3.5 million for the Hormel Gay and Lesbian Center at the San Francisco Public Library. Since coming out, Chuck has had a keen interest in supporting LGBT literature and preserving LGBT history.Chuck had the good fortune to come out in 1972 in the most supportive possible environment. Michael A. Schoch, his partner of eighteen years, succumbed to AIDS in 1994. Chuck has been living with HIV since 1987.